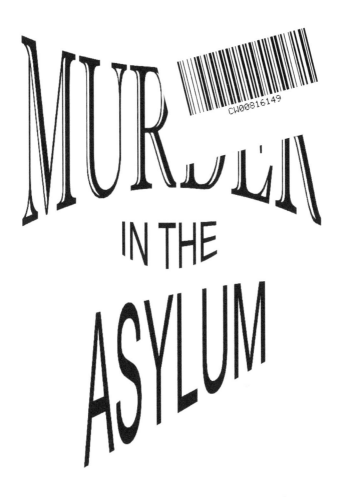

MURDER
IN THE
ASYLUM

A Novel By

Jacqueline Opresnik

ISBN 978-1-7774328-1-2 e-book

ISBN 978-1-7774328-2-9 book

Cover designed by Sandra Muzyka

For Sandy, who thought this would make an

interesting story.

Other Books

by

Jacqueline Opresnik

The Misha Plate

How to Make Money Flowers

Package from the Past

In Search of Jeremy Griffin

The Grants of Maxwell Street

The Grants at War

The Hunt for William Williamson

Chapter 1

"Well, what do you think?" Kit leveled the painting as the wire on the back of it moved on a screw that the previous owner had fortunately centred above the fireplace with another piece of artwork in mind. She let the bottom edge of the frame rest gently against the wall and stood back to admire her latest acquisition.

"I love the picture but I'm not sure about the frame," said Pat. Her friend surveyed the living room with its various shades and tones of rusty-red and cream, with accents of black. "The colour is all right and fits in, but it's a bit plain and old looking."

Kit looked at the oil painting of ships and sea with a critical eye. Purchased at an estate sale, the subject with its muted colours of blues and greens in the sky and sea had appealed to her eye, but now attention focused on the plain, black wooden frame, with its dented edges and faded paint in spots along the bottom.

Kit placed her wine glass on the coffee table and sat next to her friend, considering the picture. "I'll have to move this lamp a bit, or maybe get a different shade," she said, gesturing toward the tall floor lamp next to Pat. "There's a bit of a glare."

"Maybe it would look better if it had a mat around the edge," suggested Pat. "Or a more substantial frame," she added. "It's a large picture after all." Then reconsidering, "Then again, maybe just a thin metal frame."

Kit leaned back on the couch and surveyed the picture in its place above the fireplace, that already seemed to fit into the décor of the room.

"I wonder what year it was painted," asked Pat. "It looks very old. It looks like it might be the original frame as well."

"I asked that question, when I paid for it." Kit took a sip of wine, keeping the glass in her hand as she answered, pushing her dark hair back with her free hand. "The estate sale manager didn't know a lot about the painting, except that it had been in the possession of the Northwood family for many years. He did know that the Northwoods came from England, but that's all. It doesn't seem to have a signature, we checked and there was nothing on the back to suggest a name either. I suppose one of the family could have painted it."

"Hmm," said Pat, after swallowing. "A framing shop might recognize the artist."

"Maybe, most do offer prints for sale as well as frames. I'm off at noon, so I'll go tomorrow. There's one store close by on Scott Street."

"How was your last day yesterday?" asked Pat.

"Well, it wasn't actually my last day. I have a couple of days next week then I start my vacation for two weeks. It will be nice to get to work on the house full time for a while." A thought occurred to her and she laughed thinking of the joke they played on the purchase manager before she left.

"You should have seen Harold's face when I showed him the new design that we approved. It was a 1920s dress with the waist dropped down to the hips. I chose the gaudiest colours I could find for it. The look on his face when I told him we'd start production immediately in plus sizes only."

Pat laughed, envisioning the interchange between them. She heard stories of Harold—a Stan Laurel type of a man in both appearance and manner—and could only imagine his reaction. "I hope you let him in on the joke before you left."

Kit, still giggling, continued, "Then Larry came in with a load of fabric samples, all sheer. After a gasp of disbelief from Harold, Shari came in with the rest of the staff carrying a birthday cake, singing. Finally realizing it was a gag he relaxed, but just a little." They both laughed.

"It sounds like something you'd think up," said Pat.

Pat was her best friend and lived at the other end of town about ten minutes away from the new home Kit had moved into just a month ago. She had helped Kit with the usual cleaning and painting one does when you buy a new home and Kit was grateful for her help and expertise in decorating.

The living room was as complete as it was going to get for the time being; the oil painting filling up the empty space on the wall was the finishing touch.

"I like it," said Kit. "It's almost, like stepping into a time in the past." She looked fondly at the scene of various sized boats in a crowded harbour and wondered, what size was a boat before it was considered to be a ship? There was a long stretch of wide, pebbled road along the side of the harbour where men were unloading cargo, fixing nets, or selling fish to the many servants

3

who came down to buy the fresh catch-of-the-day for their households. She was glad she had gone to the estate sale with her friend, and glad now too she had found the painting.

◆ ◆ ◆

The door chime sounded, indicating someone had entered the store. Mike glanced up from the framed baseball jersey he was wrapping for his customer and watched as a tall, young woman entered the shop.

Seeing the only clerk in the shop was busy, Kit set down the package she was carrying—the large rectangular painting, carefully wrapped in a protective green garbage bag—by the front window and feigned interest in the works of art offered for sale along the wall of the shop until he had completed his sale.

"I'm sure your husband will like this gift, Mrs. Kramar," said Mike, taping the final open-end of the wrapping closed. His fingers slipped and the tape twisted before he could fasten the paper. He glanced at the young woman as he removed the tape from around his finger, relieved she hadn't noticed, then tried again with a fresh piece. Mrs. Kramer followed his gaze and smiled to herself.

The young woman—her long, brown hair released from the hood of her coat, curled about her shoulders—continued along the wall of available framed art. She wore a long, black trench coat, trimmed in tan, slightly damp from the drizzle that had persisted most of the day. Mrs. Kramar noticed how the woman's boots and crossbody handbag matched her ensemble. She smiled at the young woman as she left the shop, clutching the birthday present she had had framed for her husband.

Mike came from behind the counter and approached the wrapped painting. "You've brought something to be framed?" he asked.

Kit turned and smiled. "Yes," she said, coming over to him and picking up the painting. "I bought it at an estate sale. I'm afraid the frame is quite old, so I hope there will be no problem putting on a new one." Pulling the plastic bag away, Mike helped her lay the painting on the worktable. "I think it deserves something nicer."

Her eyes were a deep, navy blue he noticed, with flecks of a lighter blue.

"Hmm," said Mike. "You're right. It is a beautiful painting." He leaned over the picture looking for a signature. "It looks very much like a Webb; I've always liked his harbour scenes. An English painter, I believe, nineteenth century. Many of his paintings are of ships, but it might be by a different artist, there doesn't seem to be a signature."

He ran his hand along the edge of the frame, feeling the gouges and dents, the result of years of wear. "I think we can find something worthy of it. Do you have a preference as to metal or wood?"

"Either is okay, as long as it goes with my room." She fished out her phone from her purse. "Here, I took some pictures before I came over so you could see the colour scheme."

Kit handed him the phone so he could enlarge the photos. "Well, the black frame that's already on it does fit well with your colours and it does make the painting stand out. I see you have it above the fireplace." He wondered if the fireplace was a working wood fireplace. "You might consider glass too as an option. It will protect the painting from smoke over time, but then I'd recommend a mat as well, so the glass doesn't directly touch the paint."

Kit glanced at the photo he was looking at. "It's a gas fireplace, do I still need glass?"

"No, it's not necessary but still an option. This is a fairly large painting, though, so you might also want to consider how many more inches a mat and frame would add."

"Okay, well, let's say no glass then, just a frame. Do you think a plain black metal frame would look good?"

"Yes. That or a narrow wooden frame of a complimentary colour. Let's go over and look at the samples." He motioned to the workbench at the back of the store.

Mike picked up the painting and carried it over to the workstation where the wall behind it held samples of all the frames the store offered; each kind made up illustrating how a corner would look.

"I like that one," said Kit. Mike reached up and pulled the selected wooden frame corner off from its Velcro fastening.

"You've got a good eye." He placed the sample along the edge of the painting, the dark charcoal colour matching beautifully with the stone harbour front. The narrow edge sculpted but not ornate. "I like it too, and it will go with your colours. It will frame the work nicely without drawing your eye away from it.

"Good," said Kit. "Then, that's the one."

With the selection process over, Kit opened her purse intending to pay. "How much will it be all together?"

Mike pulled out the drawer of the table and took out a measuring tape, and calculator. After taking the dimensions and frame information he figured out the cost of the frame. He entered the numbers into his calculator and wrote the amount down. "Seventy-two-forty, plus tax," he said finally. "That's eighty-one-eighty."

"That will be fine. When can I pick it up?"

He smiled, glad that he would be seeing her again. "Tomorrow, I close at noon on Saturdays, so, say around eleven." He picked up the painting and carried it over to the order desk. "I'll need your name and phone number," he said while turning the page of his order book to a fresh entry.

"Kit," said Kit, hesitating, waiting for a response before finishing with her last name.

"Kit?"

She smiled. She'd played this game many times; new acquaintances intrigued by her name, and was prepared. "Yes, I'm named after my great, grandmother. It's also a nickname for Kathleen."

He nodded in understanding. "So, your name is really Kathleen."

"No, it's Kit."

"You're named after your great, grandmother, whose name was Kathleen, but your name isn't Kathleen."

"Right, but her given name was actually Alice not Kathleen, they just called her Kit." He looked puzzled and set the pen down. Then she laughed, deciding to enlighten him. "Her last name was Carson, so … Kit Carson, you know the famous frontiersman."

Mike smiled, realizing that this was a jest often played out. "Yes, I've heard of him. I take it, your last name isn't Carson." He waited to see if there was another story to go along with her last name.

"No, it's Morrison."

He smiled. "Well, Miss Morrison, I'm Mike Reynolds, and I'll have your picture ready for you tomorrow."

Chapter 2

Kit pulled up to the parking space in front of the shop's window, and got out, careful of the puddles that had been created by a night and morning of soft rain. It was sunny now, but the air was crisp. Kit glanced at the window and could see the owner near the order desk at the back of the store.

Mike Reynold's Frames—the sign above the door said. The chime sounded briefly as she opened the glass door then ceased as it was closed.

Mike looked up from what he was doing and waved a greeting. He smiled as she approached the counter then saw the reaction in her eyes as she noticed her painting hanging up on the wall behind the desk, giving her a realistic view as opposed to seeing it on the counter before it was wrapped.

Kit smiled in return. "I love it. It will look great on my wall."

"I'm glad. I like it too."

She approached the desk as he took down the painting. She noticed his dark hair and hazel eyes and the muscles in his arms as he lowered the picture, and wondered why she hadn't noticed how attractive he was yesterday.

Mike tore off a length of manilla paper from the roll attached to the side of the table and began wrapping the painting. "I wrapped up the old frame for you too," he said. "I thought as it was possibly the original, you might want to keep it."

"That was thoughtful, thank you." Kit opened the side pocket of her purse and drew out her credit card.

"There's something else I thought a little strange, though," he added. Mike pulled a file folder out from the drawer in the side of the desk and placed it on the paper. He opened the folder and gently took out a newspaper clipping. It was brown with age and fragile, placed inside a plastic sleeve of a page protector. "It's from 1868. I found it pressed against the painting before the back cardboard had been put on." He turned the plastic towards Kit so she could read the article headlined: *Murder of a Lunatic*.

"It's from a Yorkshire paper but describes a murder that happened in a lunatic asylum in Essex. I thought you might want to preserve it, seeing it seems to be part of the picture's history."

"Thank you. I wonder why it was kept inside the painting? Maybe the original owner was a relative," suggested Kit. "It obviously meant a lot to someone."

It looked like the clipping her grandfather had kept about her grandmother's passing; her obituary; carefully cut and separated from the rest of the paper. He had kept it in a small box in his bedroom in memory, aged now too, to a pale mottled brown. She had kept the clipping in a small photo album along with other personal documents that had belonged to her grandparents and a small pang of sadness came over her as she turned the plastic around to read.

'*Murder of a Lunatic*', was the heading, and below that, a tale of betrayal and death in an English asylum. '*April 23, 1868. William Warren Martin, an inmate in*

10

the Creighton Lee Asylum was murdered Saturday, having been struck on the head with a shovel, by a fellow inmate. Two attendants on duty that morning heard loud cries from several men in the garden area. They found the body of William Martin on the ground, bleeding, his head having been crushed by a shovel wielded by another inmate who was standing over the body, ready to strike the man again. Martin, a fisherman from Barking, died later that evening. According to the asylum administration, the two men had been best friends and often sat together discussing the Bible. An inquest is to follow.'

"Sad, isn't it?" said Mike. "To have your only friend in the world kill you like that."

Kit was silent, re-reading the article before she responded, "Yes. I wonder why he was in the asylum. I don't know anything about 19th century asylums."

"It says he was a fisherman," said Mike. "Who knows what kinds of fish you'd find in the Thames River. Wasn't it full of sewage back then?" After Kit had read the article and handed it back, he placed the protected news clipping inside the wrapping then folded the ends over and taped them. "It might be interesting to find out though," he offered. "I've always loved history, and this has a hint of mystery about it."

He'd piqued her curiosity now. "This might make an interesting story," Kit said. Then she smiled, realizing she was also becoming interested in this mysterious Martin. "I'd like to know more about him too. Do you think there might be records somewhere about him?"

Mike took Kit's credit card and entered the required information, then handed the debit machine back to her so she could enter her pin. "I helped my father a few years ago with our family genealogy and at that time there were census records as well as birth, marriage and death records. There should be more online now. He was a fisherman, so maybe there are records about that as well."

Kit removed her card from the machine, then handed it back to Mike. Her picture wrapped; Kit thanked Mike for his help with the painting. "I think I will go home and see what I can find on the internet."

He picked up the wrapped painting and old frame. "I'll help you out with this." Then added hopefully, "I have the rest of the day off if you'd like some company. I could help with the search."

Kit hesitated, but just for a second before replying. She was attracted to this man and it might be fun to work on a project together. "I'd like that," she said, then added, "and I'm sure my roommate won't mind us setting up in the dining room."

She took a pen from her purse and quickly wrote down her address. "About an hour, then?"

He smiled. "That'll give me time to close up. I'll bring my laptop too." He closed the door of her trunk where the painting lay on a folded blanket to prevent it from moving around when the car stopped. He waited until she had fastened her seatbelt before closing her door for her.

Kit rolled down her window once the car had started and smiled. "See you then."

Once on the road, Kit engaged her car phone and made a call to her friend Pat. "Hi, are you free for a few hours. Okay, I'd like you to hang around my house this afternoon for a while and pretend to be my roommate. No, I'm not joking, I … well, I've invited the guy from the framing shop to stop by and work on a project with me, and because I don't really know him, I thought … Good, see you soon."

❖ ❖ ❖

Kit sat in her favourite chair by the window, watching the street, with a warm mug of tea in her hands. Pat had arrived shortly after she had parked her car in the driveway making sure to move up to allow room for two more vehicles.

Thoroughly briefed she stood next to Kit now, eagerly awaiting the mystery man Kit had told her about. Pat leaned over the back of Kit's chair, straining to see down the street, then swept her fair hair back after it fell across her vision. "So, what's he like?"

"He seems very nice. He has an interest in history and like me, was intrigued by the newspaper article … and that's all there is to it," she added, in response to Pat's raised eyebrow.

"Okay, what's my role? Just so I know."

Kit smiled at her friend. "You're my roommate, who may or may not stick around, depending on how things go."

"Got it. Make myself scarce, but still be here." She took another glance out the window. "Good thing I brought some work with me. I need to get that design for Mrs. Wagner done by tomorrow."

13

"Oh, here's a car slowing down." Kit handed back the mug, and moved away from the window.

Mike parked on the street opposite her house, and waved once he noticed Kit at the front door.

She held the screen open for him, his arms full, carrying a large leather satchel and a roll of kraft paper; the kind he used for wrapping up customer's pictures.

Mike saw her glance at the roll of paper. "I thought we might use this to map out a timeline in our discoveries and make some notes as we find things relevant."

He glanced at Pat standing behind Kit, having noticed her for the first time. He smiled. "Hi, I'm Mike Reynolds."

"Oh," said Kit, embarrassed now at not introducing her friend right off. "This is my friend Pat Morgan."

"Mike was the one who put the new frame on the painting," she added.

"Hi." Pat reached across to take the roll of paper from him. *So, friend was it. What happened to roommate? It seemed the roommate scenario was being replaced at the last minute by the friend, who will probably leave earlier than planned scenario.* She smiled. That was okay, she still had work she could do in the meantime.

"You made good time; closing up, I mean, then going home."

He smiled. "I didn't have far to go. I live in one of the apartments above the store. When I bought the building, I took the smaller of the two and rented the other one to a nice Dutch couple. They're good

14

tenants…" then added, "and occasionally they invite me over for supper."

The foyer was small and self-contained, with a tall radiator and deacon's bench on opposite walls. A door opened into the living room. Mike sat on the deacon's bench, preparing to replace his runners for the extra pair of shoes he'd brought.

"Your runners are fine," said Kit.

He smiled. "You're sure? My mother always said, 'never assume'."

"Well, I appreciate that, but you're fine. Come on, we'll set up on the dining room table, there's more room there."

He followed Kit into the adjacent living room, then saw the picture he had framed up on the wall above the fireplace. He stopped, wanting to appreciate the painting. "It looks great there, and the frame you chose is perfect."

Before Kit could respond, Pat joined them again. "I'll work in the other room. I've got some phone calls to make too," she said. She quickly glanced at the clock in the dining room. "I don't suppose you two have had lunch yet. Why don't I make us some sandwiches, while you get yourselves organized."

Mike smiled at the thought of food. "That would be nice. Thank you, Pat."

Pat scurried off to the kitchen leaving them to set up. Suddenly on their own, Kit sensed a shyness about their new friend.

"Come on. We can set up on the table over here."

He nodded, and carrying his satchel, followed her to the dining room.

"There's a plug on that wall," she said, pointing to the receptacle behind his chair. "I'm sure our batteries will run out before we get very far."

Kit noticed him looking around the room. "This is very nice. Have you lived here long?" he asked.

"I moved in a month ago. Pat's been wonderful helping me clean and decorate."

"I should be," called Pat from the kitchen. "It's my job after all."

Kit laughed. "True. She's an interior decorator," she added.

"Well, your photos didn't do the living room justice. And the painting … You know, I read that newspaper clipping at least four times before you came to pick up the painting. I kept thinking, there has to be more to it, the story I mean. Why was he in the asylum? Who put him there? Did he have family? How was he treated? What do people fish for in Kent?" He smiled sheepishly realizing he'd been going on. Maybe she didn't share his enthusiasm.

"Do you think we can find out much more?"

Mike turned on his laptop, then making sure the transformer was positioned under his chair, plugged the cord into the wall plug. "We can try. I helped my father a few years ago with our family tree, I remember some of the sites we used. The internet has a lot of information. I'm sure we'll find something."

"All right. Where do we start?"

He sat down opposite Kit, waiting for her to turn on her machine. "I've been thinking about that too. I suppose we start with the article about his death and see how much we can figure out from that, then go backwards from there."

"Here we go," announced Pat, setting down a small tray with two plates, each displaying a ham sandwich with a dollop of mustard on the side, two small bottles of soda and some napkins. "All you had left in the fridge was orange soda," she said, defending her lack of choice in beverage. "You're all out of coffee and you have one teabag left, that I knew you'd want for your breakfast tomorrow."

Kit gave her a look. "The orange will be fine, Pat. And thank you for making us lunch."

Pat gave her an exaggerated smile. "I'll go work in the other room. I have everything I need on my tablet anyway." Tray in hand, Pat went off into the family room that adjoined both the kitchen and the dining room, leaving Kit and Mike to work together on their own; close but not too close.

Chapter 3

They ate their meal while setting up the area, sitting opposite each other along the sides of the wooden table; a long piece of kraft paper that Mike had torn off the roll, then folded to prevent damage to the table, lay lengthwise before them.

Kit smiled at Mike as she opened the folder and took out the clipping, eager to begin. She read the words carefully, stopping after a pertinent point to take notes. "Okay, we know he died," she said, then corrected herself, "or rather was murdered, April 23, 1868. He was a fisherman who lived in Barking. His name was William Martin."

Mike took another bite of his sandwich, then washed it down with soda before answering. "And we know, even though this happened in Essex, it must have been such a rare event that it was printed in many newspapers across England. Just the fact that it gained a mention in the news is interesting. Maybe asylums weren't as bad as we imagine, and this event was truly shocking for the time."

"I have visions of people being manacled to the wall and electric shock treatments being used. I suppose a lot of our preconceptions come from the way the film industry depicts the sinister doctor in thriller movies," said Kit.

"Probably. Let's see what they were really like. I'll search for Victorian asylums," suggested Mike.

"And, I'll look under, asylum life in 1860s England and see what comes up," said Kit. They sat quietly, each looking into the life that William Martin might have led during his time in the asylum. Occasionally, Kit would steal a covert glance at Mike as he searched intently at his screen. The sun from the window behind her was just starting to make a pattern on the wall; its light forming colours as it passed through the bevels of the stained glass. She liked him, even though she realized she knew little about him. He was someone she wanted to get to know.

"It seems that in the 1700s the asylums were pretty bad; they existed merely to segregate the mentally ill from the rest of the population, but at the beginning of the 1800s there was a growing compassionate view of the mentally ill and the doctors of the time sought to provide a more progressive approach to the people in their care. But then, in the mid to the end of the 1800s there was an increase in the asylum population, which created a backlash and the facilities went back to their harsh treatment in order to reduce and control the overcrowded population." Mike moved to the next site he had saved, then continued. "They could no longer provide the individualized care they had initially proposed, and the asylums became unfavourable places for the mentally ill. That's sad; they'd tried, but there were too many people and not enough resources. They reverted back to drugs and restraints to control the inmates. I suppose too, there were additional medical reasons for the increase; dementia, late-stage syphilis, or brain damage caused by alcoholic abuse." He considered their search. "I wonder why William was sent to an asylum? I suppose we'll never find out, really. Doctors' knowledge back then too was medically limited."

Kit read from a page she had found, "The Lunatic Asylums Act of 1853 laid out rules for patient admittance. Wow, the name of the act tells you something. What they actually thought of the inmates, I mean. They could have just as well called it The Asylum Act."

"I suppose to the legislators of the time, anyone in an asylum was a lunatic, insane or an imbecile."

"Well, this at least is encouraging." added Kit. "They required a medical certificate to be signed before anyone was admitted. And they also required a justice, a clergyman or an overseer to sign that order committing the person. You'd think that would stop any false commitments."

"I'm not too sure about that," said Mike. "On the dark side, once a patient was admitted, there was no way to get out. This site suggests that there seemed to be more women than men in the asylums. So, a wealthy man, tired of his wife, could simply have a doctor sign a certificate then get one of the others to agree, and off she went to an asylum. Or a young woman who spoke out of turn, wanting more freedom or education, or just defying her father or husband, could similarly be sent away to a private asylum."

Kit grimaced at that. "I don't think I'd do so well in Victorian England."

Mike laughed at her expression. "It wasn't just England."

"I know, here's a horror story that I thought was English but turns out its from America," said Kit.

"It says here that many private madhouses," she shook her head sadly, "allowed rich people to come in and watch the inmates after paying an admission fee. They could taunt and throw things at the patients which added to their entertainment. There was also a lot of speculation by doctors as to why people were insane and some doctors eagerly performed post mortems on dead inmates thinking they could see somewhere in the brain, proof of their theories. I'm not reading a lot of cruelty in asylums, but I'm sure, like in any profession of authority there were staff members that mistreated the people under their care. This site talks about people being chained to their beds, living in straight jackets and medical procedures such as cupping, blistering and bleeding, but these are mostly spoken of in the 1700s. I know what bleeding is, but what are cupping and blistering?"

Mike hesitated. He'd read about this a long time ago and wasn't too sure how to describe it. "They take a cup and heat the inside somehow then place it on the skin. The vacuum caused by the heating causes a suction and can cause skin redness. Some therapists of alternative medicine use the technique today for pain. I'm not sure what blistering is, but it sounds dreadful."

"I'll search for it," said Kit. It took a moment until she found a site that explained the procedure "I found something here. I can't believe anyone could even come up with this. They make a plaster out of dead Spanish flies and apply it to the skin. The heat caused blisters.

The thinking was, that it burned out the disease. I wonder why, are Spanish flies hotter than other flies? And where do you get Spanish flies in England?" She shook her head thinking of importing flies from Spain.

Mike sat back in his chair and rubbed his eyes. They'd been looking at their respective computers for over two hours. "There should be some record somewhere about William Martin. The Act said too that there had to be a record of the person upon entering an asylum with all their personal information."

Kit nodded in agreement. "So, where do we start?"

Mike thought for a moment. "There are some free sites we can use to check for census records, and we can check historical records for information about fishing during the Victorian era."

Kit smiled, eager to begin. "Okay, point me to a census site. He died in 1868, so maybe he is on a Barking census record."

"True, the records start in 1841 and go up in ten-year increments. I would start looking in 1861. Here, go to Family Search, it's a free site we can use."

Kit searched for the site, then waited while the page came up. We have to 'register or login'," she said.

"I'm already registered there. It's free, so you can register later if you like." He quickly wrote down his email address and his password. "Here's my login information. While you do that, I think I will check out the town of Barking and see what I can find."

Once logged in, Kit selected the 'search all records' option and put in the few facts they knew; his name and possible residence in 1861. "What should I put for his year of birth?" she asked. "The article doesn't give his age."

"Hmm. That's true, he might have been old or young. Asylums didn't have age requirements. Try 1790 to 1850, that should cover it."

Kit started to fill in the dates. "Oh, and leave the birthplace blank," he added. "Then when the results come up, you can search through them and start to look for the records in Essex, just in case he lived there then."

The page came up and Kit scrolled to the bottom of the page, glancing at the results as she did. "Oh, my," she said. "There are more than ten pages of Martin results." She clicked on page ten, then continued until she had reached page forty-five. "Wrong, there are over forty-nine pages."

Mike smiled at her reaction. "Not to worry, we can narrow it down a bit."

Kit sighed. "Thank goodness. How?"

"Look at the top of the page for the 'collections' tab. Click on that and you will see; below the birth, marriage, death section, there is a census section. Choose the 1861 census as a filter."

He came around the table to stand next to Kit as she made the selection. He leaned forward to touch the screen, pointing out the place to click on. He could smell the shampoo she had used recently and was suddenly happy that she had invited him to help her with the search. Focused once more, he snorted with amusement when he saw the page. "Looks like 'Martin' is a very common name. So, we may have to put Essex in under the residence information and see if we can narrow that down a bit. If there are still a lot, we can add Barking and see what comes up. Don't forget to check for W. Martin as well, they usually show up towards the end."

He went back to his chair and smiled at their efforts. They each worked quietly, engrossed in their respective search, as the living room clock struck three.

"I found a neat site about the fishermen of Barking," said Mike. "It says, that Barking once had the largest fishing fleet in the world. It seemed that the most industrious years began in the 1800s. In 1805, there were twenty-three smacks in Barking. By 1811 there were forty, and by 1850 they had 220 fishing boats."

Kit listened as he read the information. "What are smacks?"

"Must be some kind of fishing boat. I'll see what more I can find out."

There was an exclamation from the other room. "Yes, got it!" Pat came into the room, a triumphant look on her face. "I got the contract," she said. Then, as if just remembering something important, she looked around, patting her pockets, her triumph turning to panic. "My keys. I can't find my keys. I have an appointment in half an hour."

Kit laughed. "Try the coatrack."

Relieved, Pat went to the foyer and then waved a farewell. "Thanks. I'll call you later."

"Wow. I like your friend." Mike laughed at her animated exit.

"She does get excited, doesn't she. I've known Pat since we were five in Kindergarten. She's always been there for me."

Kit focused back on her task. "I've gone through all the names on the 1861 census and only found two in Essex and neither was a fisherman. So, I'm going back to 1851, now."

Knowing Kit could now manipulate the filters on her own, Mike acknowledged her results, then grew silent as he read more about Barking. Discovering something interesting, he said, "This is amazing. And here I thought they only fished in the Thames or Channel. An entrepreneur had the idea to couple faster boats with the fishing boats that were often as far away as Iceland. Because it wasted time for the fishing boats to return home to sell their catch, faster boats called 'cutters' would bring supplies and ice, take the caught and iced fish from the fishermen, then sail home quickly to sell them, leaving the fishermen to stay where they were, often for months at a time. Very smart."

"Yes, but it must have been a harsh life, living on a fishing boat for that long."

"True, I don't think I could do that."

They worked in companionable silence each with their thoughts about the man they were seeking.

"I think I found him. Look." Kit waited as Mike came to her side, then pointed to the results before clicking on the actual document. "Here, he's listed as a visitor, visiting another fisherman by the same last name. By their ages; William fifty-nine and George sixty-one, I would think this George might be his brother."

"Where was William born?"

Kit scrolled right, over to the birth location information. "Dartford, Kent. He and George both."

"I think you're right. It says he's married too. I wonder where his family is?"

"We have his age now, so I can go and look for the birth records in Dartford."

"Very good. I'm going to look up 'smacks' and see what they were." He gave her shoulder a pat in congratulations before going back to his computer. His touch was brief and friendly, but she felt it, as if it were electric. She smiled as he sat back down, trying not to stare, but wanting to look at him. His enthusiasm was contagious and she carried on looking for the birth records of the two brothers.

"I don't believe this; how could a clergyman actually enter this into the records?" said Kit.

Mike looked up wondering what she had found.

"Here is a birth for a George Kirby, son of George Edward Kirby of London a wine merchant, and Anita Brown of Barking, concubine. Wow, is that the same as a mistress?" Kit laughed. "I wonder what the boy would think if he grew up and ever saw his birth certificate?"

Mike smiled. "Very interesting, I can't say I've ever heard of anything like that before. We'll probably find a lot of interesting things before we're done."

"Oh, I found him and his brother! I just entered the last name, date and Dartford then several came up. William Warren Martin was born June 3, 1792 and christened June 4, 1792 and George Thomas born April 10, 1789, christened June 4, 1792. The parents were William and Sarah. There is a younger sister named

Mary and another brother Edward, who were also christened in 1792."

"Well done," said Mike, amazed at how quickly she had found out the information they were seeking. "Sometimes you will see that. Where a family moves somewhere and has all the children baptised at the local church at the same time."

He rose from his chair and pointed toward the painting on the wall. Curious, Kit joined him. "And *I* found out something. That my friend, is a 'smack'. The Barking smacks had a unique, red ochre colour in the sails. The canvas was left to weather before the cream colour was dyed the reddish colour."

"So, it seems that this is a picture of part of the Barking fishing fleet." She counted the number of red and cream sails in the harbour. "I wonder if the Northwoods were actually related to the fisherman?"

"Hard to say. We may find out eventually." They walked back to the dining room table, each to their side, prepared now to hunt for the fisherman's family.

The sun's first rays hit the west facing wall of the dining room window. Its light reflected through the bevelled edge of the glass, casting a coloured rainbow on to the wall next to Mike.

They'd sat for over three hours, searching and it was beginning to get late. "Shall we take a break?" suggested Kit. "I'll see what I can rustle up for supper. That is if you'd care to stay."

The rainbow lines flinched at the movement of a shrub outside.

"I'd like nothing better," he said, smiling. "I'd like to wash my hands first."

She nodded toward the small hallway behind him, that led to the downstairs washroom. "Just to the right."

Once in the kitchen, she opened the doors to her storage cupboards one at a time, wondering what she could make for their supper, wishing now she'd gone shopping on the way home. She then next went to the freezer section of the fridge. She had hamburger patties, but no buns.

Mike joined her at the counter that divided the kitchen area into two sections. Normally an area used for eating, Kit had set up a couch and two chairs where guests could relax and still talk to her while she worked in the kitchen. She noticed him looking around the room.

"Maybe one day I'll take out the wall between this room and the dining room and bring the dining room table back into this area, making it a more open space, then I can use the wall space for more cabinets, but for now I like the coziness of this arrangement."

"I like it," he said. "It works well, giving it a cozy feeling. It's nice to be able to talk to your guests while you cook."

She opened the cupboard above the microwave as a last hope of finding something suitable. "I want to change the hardware too." She placed her hand into the cupboard handle again to demonstrate how small the opening was. "I don't have the right kind of screwdriver, all I have is a flat-edged one."

Mike smiled. "You mean a slot screwdriver."

"Yes, and I need a pointy-shaped one.

"A Phillips," he said

She laughed. "Yes, I guess. What's the square one called?"

"A Robertson. There's actually another one called a Torx. It's a star-shaped one." He came around the counter and looked at the hinge screws. "I have quite a collection of tools," he said. "I could help you take the doors off. You might have a difficult time replacing the handles using the same screw holes, though. The newer handles have a slightly longer length between the holes."

Kit looked closer at the handles then gave him a questionable look. "I don't suppose you have a drill too?"

"Of course. But in the mean time, why don't I order us a pizza for supper. Then we can continue with our search while we wait."

Kit gave a sigh. She hadn't planned on company and up till now had kept only a few necessities. "That would be perfect. Thanks."

m◆ ◆ ◆

"We know his birth date, so let's look for a marriage, probably in Barking. So, start with" –Mike made a quick calculation— "1808 to 1828 in Barking and see what comes up."

Kit entered the new information and watched as the results came onto the screen. A William Martin married in 1804, Barking, was the first one she checked. The transcript came up and she made note of the information, even though this William was too young. Then to the right, she noticed that the information came

29

from a site that was available for browsing. "Look at this! I can go on this site and view all of the birth, death and marriage records from Barking, from the 1500s to the 1900s. The actual entries, that's amazing."

Mike smiled at her enthusiasm. He was enjoying his time and glad now he had suggested the collaboration.

Her phone suddenly came alive making a vibrating, buzzing sound—a call. She checked to see if Pat was calling, then answered. "Hello. Yes. Yes, Mr. Jenkins." Mike watched as she took the call, her face showing a puzzled response to the voice at the other end. "I don't think so. I rather like it. I'm sorry. Okay, goodbye."

Mike raised an eyebrow in expectation as she concluded the call. "That was Mr. Jenkins, the man from the estate sale. He wants to buy my painting back. He says he got a wire from the nephew of Ralph Northwood, who lives in England. He wants to buy it back from me because he has fond memories of it in their home when he was young. He wasn't able to get here in time for the sale."

"That's unusual."

"Yes, that, and the fact he offered me five hundred dollars for it."

"Wow. What are you thinking of doing?"

"I'm not sure now. It does seem a shame that it means something to the family, but it's starting to mean something to me too, besides, it looks great in my home."

"I suppose, if the Northwoods had wanted him to have it, they would have left it to the nephew with other valuables they had, in the Will."

"You know, you're right. How do we know what they thought of him. The Northwoods lived in this country, for a while at least, and must have left other items to other people."

The tune of Beethoven's Fifth announced the arrival of their pizza. "I'll go," said Mike, leaving Kit to her thoughts about the painting.

Kit was standing in front of the art work when Mike entered the room with a large flat pizza box. "I do like it, very much," she said. "I really don't want to sell it."

"I'm glad." He smiled at her decision. He admired the picture once again, then raised a shoulder inviting her to come and enjoy their supper.

Kit picked up her second piece of pizza. "This, is so good. I didn't realize how hungry I was." They sat opposite each other at the kitchen counter. Her side of the bar didn't have the overhang Mike's side had, so she sat sideways to avoid banging her knees.

"You know, I've had a great time today," said Mike. "If I was at home, I'd probably be working in the shop; tidying up or working on an order. But being here, looking into the story of the fisherman, gave the day a new purpose." He smiled at her; glad the phone call's effects had lessened, as he picked up his next slice. "It's more enjoyable to work on things with someone else. Even when I was working on our family history with my dad, there were days I worked alone and it wasn't as much fun." He took a bite then considered. "Now that he's gone, I think maybe it was just because we were working on something together. Maybe it wouldn't have mattered what it was. Just that we were having fun together."

"True. I used to love making bird houses with my dad when I was little." She took a lingering bite on her slice of pizza.

"I think we'll find out more about William Martin … that is, if you'd like to continue."

"Yes, I would. When's a good time?"

She smiled. "You did offer to help take the cabinet doors off."

"So, I did. Tomorrow, then?

Chapter 4

Sunday morning didn't start as Kit had hoped. A storm, starting early before dawn, now whipped its fury against her dining room windows, rain falling in a cascade down the glass. Mike was due after breakfast and it was close to ten now. She sat by the living room window as she had done yesterday, waiting, watching as the wind drove the rain at an angle. With the lake effect altering the severity of the storm here, she wondered if Pat was experiencing the same storm at her house ten minutes away, which in turn reminded her of her deception. She would have to tell Mike that Pat wasn't really a roommate; but a good friend who lived not too far away.

Kit heard the sound of her cellphone as it vibrated on the table next to her. She glanced to check who was calling before answering. It was the same number as yesterday—Jenkins. "Yes?" She switched the phone to her other hand so she could readily see down the street between the vertical blinds. "Yes, Mr. Jenkins. I've decided to keep the picture. Yes, I realize five-hundred is a generous offer, but … Please, let your client know… I'm sorry but I intend to keep it. No, raising the price won't change my mind. Okay, yes, if I reconsider, I have your number."

She recognized his car; a modest model of quite a few years, as it slowed down at the corner, then pulled into her driveway. An umbrella emerged first as he got out stepping gingerly; trying to avoid any puddles in the driveway caused by depressions in the interlock, and climbed the steps to her door.

Kit opened the door without waiting for the doorbell and smiled at his dishevelled look. He saw her glance, then took in his own appearance; dirt and grease on his jeans, his damp hair and rolled up sleeves. He looked sheepishly at her, shaking his umbrella out the door. "I had a flat on the way over. I'm afraid I'm a little worse for wear."

"You look fine," she said, "just a little frayed around the edges." He sat and changed his wet shoes for the ones he had brought. "Why don't you go and tidy up, you know where the bathroom is. There are extra towels on the shelf. While you're doing that, I'll make us some hot tea."

He gave her a warm smile. "Thank you, I'd like that."

Several minutes later Mike joined her in the kitchen, looking more himself and less wet thanks to her hairdryer.

"Lemon or milk?"

"Milk, please. And two sugars," he added. "That's only the second tire I've ever changed, and both on that car. I've got it down to a science now. Although it's a little more difficult doing it in the rain."

He looked handsome, she thought; more rugged and somehow more capable. Not the quiet academic he seemed yesterday.

Mike took a sip of tea, the hot cup warming his hands. "So, when shall we tackle the cupboard doors?"

"Now, if you'd like. Did you remember your tools?"

"Yes, they're out in the car." Mike finished the last of his tea. He smiled at her, eager to be of help. "I'll get them." Then a thought occurred to him. "Maybe I should park on the road and leave room for Pat's car."

"Um … about that. I should have told you before … it's actually interesting …"

"Pat, doesn't live here." He raised his eyebrows suggesting he was right and smiled softly. "It's okay. If I were a woman who lived alone and invited a stranger to come to my house, I'd probably do the same thing."

Kit let out the breath she had been holding, with a sigh. "Thanks, for understanding."

"I'll be right back."

Kit tidied up and got her small step ladder from the back sunroom, ready to help hold the doors as they were unscrewed from the cabinet.

Mike had brought his drill and several bits that easily withdrew the screws that had been in place, for who knew how long. Kit held the doors firmly against the cabinet frame as Mike loosened each hinge. Then together, they lowered the doors one at a time and set them against the wall next to the bar. Working together, it didn't take more than a half hour to remove the doors, which gave the kitchen a sudden empty look, that and the fact that Kit had few food items on the shelves, which now stood open and unfilled. But thanks to Pat's early morning delivery, the fridge was well supplied and Kit was prepared for an afternoon meal.

The sky was a light gray now and the rain continued, but with less velocity than earlier. The dining room therefore was darkened by the lack of window light and Kit turned on the stained-glass ceiling lamp that hung over the table.

The sheet of manilla was where it was yesterday, with just the death details filled in, and they continued their research where they had left off. "I suppose I can fill in his birth records now," suggested Kit.

"I think that's a safe bet, but remember, this so far is circumstantial. If we were doing an actual genealogy, we'd need to verify everything, somehow tie in the fisherman from the asylum to what we have found. Maybe we'll get some more information once you find his family."

"I forgot to tell you." She closed the lid of her laptop so she could talk more directly. "Jenkins called me again, trying to get me to sell the painting. He offered me eight-hundred dollars."

Mike looked at her in disbelief. "Why would he do that? What's so important about that painting. I don't think anyone famous painted it. I couldn't make out a signature anywhere."

"I told him I intend to keep it. He wasn't happy, but accepted my decision."

"Let's hope he doesn't call again." He caught her gaze and looked back into her eyes. Her dark hair, a halo about her shoulders, now that the sun had just reappeared from behind a cloud and lit up the window behind her. He averted his eyes back to the page he had found, affecting interest in it rather than her.

He brightened suddenly realizing he'd actually found something relevant. "This is interesting. I think I've found our William on an 1801 Dartford census. I never knew there were census records going back that far. Maybe some cities did their own census." Unable to resist the tease of further information, Kit came to his side of the table to view the page. She saw the five names listed under the name Martin: William, George, Mary, Geoffrey, and a David.

"Mike, look, they're all in a poorhouse. William, George and Mary could be from one family. I haven't seen the Geoffrey or David names before. Do you think their parents are dead?"

"Could be, but sometimes the parents just couldn't afford to keep the children. It was often a choice between starvation or the workhouse."

"What were those dates again, their birth dates?"

Kit looked at the notes made on the manilla paper, the black ink outlining a family. "William would be ten, George, twelve, and Mary nine, if they are the same family."

She looked back at his screen, amazed too that some areas had such early census records. "Do you know much about poorhouses? And are they the same as workhouses?"

"Not much, other than they were not pleasant places. I think 'poorhouse' was a term they used when it was operated by the local parish for the poor, while 'workhouse' was more of a government run institution for the poor and homeless. But there has to be a lot on the internet. I think I'll look into that for a while." Mike took a screenshot of the site where he had found the census record, then opened up another window preparing to look into the workhouses of England during the nineteenth century.

"I know we don't have conclusive proof that the workhouse people are the same as the ones I found, after all Martin is a pretty common name, but I think I will make note of the Dartford census on our timeline." Kit was filling in the record information, as Mike got her attention with something he had found.

"Um, here. I think this is a good site. Search for 'British poorhouses of the nineteenth century' then choose the second site down." Kit went back to her computer.

"Got it." She took a moment to read the article. "It says poorhouses were meant to shame people who couldn't support themselves. To punish them for being poor. It says too, that if you could work, you were expected to work in the poorhouse. They seemed to make a distinction between those who were ill and unable to look after themselves and those that could work. That was good at least."

"And if they refused to work, they could go to jail," added Mike. There was a sketch from the nineteenth century on the next page showing cramped conditions; beds, no more than coffin-sized. It explained too, that many took advantage of the workhouse in earlier times choosing to go there rather than work, then the rules changed and conditions became less than desirable. "They introduced a rule that if an able-bodied man came to a workhouse, his whole family had to go too."

"So maybe that means if the children were there alone,"—Mike gave her a cautious raised eyebrow—"I know it might not be them, but maybe that means their parents were dead."

"It's possible, but they could have gone alone too if their family couldn't feed them, or maybe they were abandoned." Then he continued, "In later years the women, men and children were separated within the workhouse, with parents allowed to see their children once a week. By the mid 1800s, workhouses often housed over a thousand people and to go to a workhouse became the ultimate indignity." He paused, "Read the next paragraph."

Kit read the next section quietly. Basically, the workhouse could sell the able-bodied inmates to local bidders or contractors in exchange for the amount it would cost to cloth and feed the individual poor person. "That's terrible. It's like being sold into slavery, with no say."

"Not a good time to be poor, that's for sure."

"I wonder if they sold the children, too?"

"I would think so; chimney sweeps, weavers; they would use small children, and I'm sure there are other professions that would as well. Yes, here. This says that the children farmed out for work, earned money for the workhouse. And workhouses often advertised for apprenticeships. They would pay an employer to take a child because it was cheaper than looking after them. One good thing, I guess, the children would have a trade eventually. I wonder if the people taking the children had to be vetted somehow. Who knows, they might have been pedophiles or worse; part of some sex trafficking ring."

"I don't think that would be the norm, after all there does seem to be some official documents involved about the arrangement, I mean if they were legally apprentices. There were rules."

"I wonder how long they had to work for the person who bought them?"

Mike, checked another site he'd found before answering. "Here's another good article as well." He scrolled down to a descriptive part. "By entering a workhouse, you were assumed to have given up the right to care for your family. Your clothing, and personal things were taken and stored for you until you left and you were given a uniform to wear. This is interesting, in one institution to shame people further; prostitutes had to wear a yellow dress and pregnant single women wore a red." He paused, "Does sound a bit like a prison doesn't it, but it does say people could leave whenever they wanted."

Kit gave a small sigh in sympathy for the children they'd found. "It does sound bleak. I wonder how long they stayed in that workhouse. I suppose there's no way of knowing."

"Maybe they were apprenticed out to someone. We may never know, or how our guy became a fisherman."

He smiled at her, his eyes a bit tired from watching the computer screen. "How about a break. The sun's been out for a while. Maybe a walk down to the pond."

"Great idea. A break would be nice."

They walked for almost fifteen minutes down the main street, shaded by tall, aged trees on either side, drips occasionally falling from the leaves. A few hundred feet more and they turned on to an old abandoned road that sloped down to the large pond, divided by a long, narrow, pedestrian bridge of metal that had been built to allow access from both sides of the pond. The far side of the bridge opened up to the other side of the old road that led up to another well-travelled road, with parking at the entrance to the now parkland area. A man and a young boy were fishing below the bridge on a weedy flat piece of land with casting access to the water.

Kit heard the boy whoop with excitement at a sharp nibble, then an, "oh, lost it" as his line slackened. The old man waved a greeting and Mike called out to ask what kind of fish they were expecting to catch.

"Hopefully, a catfish," he answered, "or maybe a carp, but we throw those ones back."

"What's a carp?" asked Kit.

Mike smiled at her question. "Just think of a giant gold fish. And I'm sure many people have let their goldfish go in the pond, when they were tired of caring for them, not wanting to kill them."

Kit laughed at that, remembering as a child the goldfish she had in a bowl above the T.V. "I wonder how big Goldie would be now if he had lived?"

"I have read that goldfish are part of the carp family and some of them can live up to thirty or forty years, and get quite large. But it's never a good idea to introduce goldfish into an ecosystem not meant for them. They are carnivorous and endanger the indigenous species by eating their eggs."

Kit gave a smile to that bit of knowledge, and wondered how Mike knew that.

They watched the two fishermen for a while before walking the remainder of the bridge. The overhanging trees gave the cracked and worn asphalt road a tunnel feeling and the dampness of the morning rain still dripped from some of the larger vegetation. The water was smooth and covered with small flies after the rain. Kit could see small circles erupt on the surface where smaller fish were enjoying the bugs.

Once up the road and out into the park area, they sat on one of the park's metal benches, enjoying the sun and watching, as cars passed by. A layer of low fog hovered over the road, as the sun's warmth hit the cooler surface. "It's turned out to be a nice day, after all," said Kit, glad now they had gone for a walk. "Do you enjoy your work?" she asked.

"What, framing? Well, I do like having my own business and I do enjoy the work. My father worked for a larger framing store, years ago. I learned the business from him. He actually helped me start up the business." He gave the explanation a slight nod. "And it does pay the bills, while I pursue my true passion."

Unable to resist Kit asked, "And what is your true passion?"

"Writing, historical fiction mostly. I couldn't get enough of history growing up."

She smiled, so that was the link. The reason the fisherman's death had triggered such an interest in him. "How many books have you written?"

"Two. I self-published them, then put them for sale as e-books on a publishing site." He gave her a sheepish look. "So far I've made $1.30 in royalties." He laughed at the thought. "Not quite enough to keep me in the lifestyle I'm accustomed to."

Kit smiled at him. "True, but that's great. It's a start. I often wished I could write. I mean, most people can write, but I mean write well and tell a great story."

"Maybe I should start writing romance novels, they seem to sell well."

She studied his face for a moment as if assessing his potential, and smiled. "Somehow, I can't picture you writing gratuitous sexy, novels."

"You're probably right," he admitted. "What do you do when you're not researching murders from the nineteenth century."

A small breeze stirred the leaves above them, shedding their few remaining drips of water. She gave a small snort at that and pushed her hair back from her eyes. "I'm a designer for a clothing firm. I wouldn't call it a passion, but it's a nice job and I get to travel a bit. When I'm not working, I enjoy puzzles, mysteries … I read a lot of mystery novels, when I'm not renovating houses."

"Hmm, I suppose our interests have drawn us together. We have discovered an historical mystery."

A sudden splash from the other side of the segmented pond, caught their attention. "What was that?"

"A fish, maybe," said Mike. "We can probably see better from the bridge."

They left the grassy area and climbed back onto the bridge to get a better look. The other side of the pond was larger and choked with vegetation, only some of it

Kit recognized as pond lilies, many in bloom with their white flowers raised up on tall stems above the leaves.

"Over there!" said Kit. Some kind of animal was swimming, causing the floating plants to part in its wake.

"A beaver, maybe," said Mike, "although I've never seen one up close before." They watched hoping to get another glimpse of the pond creature. "Yes, look." He pointed to the far bank where a domed structure of varied sized branches hugged the water's edge.

They stood on the bridge looking out over the pond, silent for a few moments, each hoping to get a glimpse of the elusive animal.

Then switching the topic from beavers back to her house, Mike said, "Speaking of renovations, do you have your paint supplies already?"

"Not yet." She gave him a quizzical look. "What are you suggesting?"

"That we go for a late lunch, then stop at a hardware store to buy what you need." Recalling the number of doors they'd taken off, and all the sanding required before painting, he added, "I can help you if you'd like."

Kit gave him a warm smile. "I'd like that very much."

He nodded at her acceptance. "Let's walk back and get my car.

Chapter 5

It was three o'clock when they arrived back at Kit's house with all the necessities needed to redo the kitchen cabinets. Pat's car was parked along the side of the road in front of the house and she was found sitting on the front-porch bench enjoying the sunshine that had stayed after the morning rain.

Pat smiled when she saw Mike's car pull into the driveway and realized the two had been together since the morning. "I'm glad you're back. Here I'll take that," she said, taking the bag of supplies from Kit as she got out of the car.

"Thanks. Why, what's up?"

"You just missed him. A tall guy with a British accent was here asking for you. I'd just arrived when a taxi stopped and he got out and called to me before I got to the door."

The paint and primer in tow, Mike gave the trunk door a push, closing it. "What did he want?"

"That's what I asked him," said Pat, more animated now with the telling. "At first he thought I was you. Once I explained, he said he wanted to speak to you about the painting you had purchased, hoping you'd changed your mind about selling it to him."

Pat led the way and held the door for them. "I don't like it," she said. "Someone just showing up like that, especially after you told the estate guy already you weren't selling."

Mike carried the paint cans to the kitchen giving the girls a chance to talk on their way in and waited, sitting at the kitchen counter.

Once they were all in the room, Mike shook his head slowly having given the mysterious man more thought. "Something doesn't seem right about this," he said. "By your description, it sounds as if the nephew has come on his own to persuade Kit. Personally, I can't see anyone going to this much trouble for a fifty-dollar painting. And I think Jenkins has probably broken some rule letting him know who you were and where you live."

Pat joined Mike at the counter while Kit unpacked the bag of items she needed for her cupboards. "I told him I'd make sure you get the message because I was your roommate." Looking mildly embarrassed, she gave Mike a guilty glance. "I didn't want him to think you lived here alone."

"It's all right," said Kit, smiling. "Mike knows."

A look of relief came over Pat. "Good. I hate secrets."

"Me too," said Mike. "I wonder what the secret is about this painting."

Kit turned to her friends and shrugged in disbelief, her hands now a little shaky. "It does seem strange. Do you think he'll get violent or break in to get it."

Mike spontaneously reached across and took one of her hands in his, for reassurance. Her hand was warm and she didn't pull away, instead finding comfort in his touch. "I doubt he'd do anything like that." Then he smiled at Pat. "It's a good thing you have a roommate to keep you company."

Kit burst out laughing at the look on Pat's face.

"I don't mind staying over," said Pat, "I can work on your upstairs next while you work on the kitchen."

"Oh, I forgot to ask you," said Kit, suddenly reminded of her friend's important meeting. "Did you get the job."

"Yes, and I don't mind telling you it is an important project; the biggest one I've had so far." She'd recovered now and didn't mind sharing the news of her success. "It's a whole house. The owner will be in Alberta for three months, so I have that much time to get it done." Then the enormity of the assignment hit her, seemingly for the first time. "That means, paint, upholstery, cabinets, flooring …" A frown clouded her face. "I'll never be able to do all that in three months."

"Sure, you will," said Kit. "And if you need help, you can call on me."

"Thanks, I may do that. So, what are you two doing this afternoon. Kitchen or research?"

"I'd like to work a bit more on looking into William Martin. What do you say Mike?"

"I'd like that too."

Pat slid off the bar stool preparing to leave. "I'll go home and get a few things then see you later tonight."

"Great. Thanks Pat."

"Bye Mike." With that she was gone, leaving the two of them to their research.

❖ ❖ ❖

They sat in their respective places at the dining room table, each deep in thought.

They worked in companionable silence until Kit broke the silence with a small whoop of success. "I think this is him. William Warren Martin married Emily Barrett May 27, 1818.

'William Warren Martin of this parish, bachelor and Emily Barrett of this same parish, spinster, were married in this church by banns, this twenty-seventh day of May, in the year one thousand, eight hundred and eighteen by me E. Elliott, curate.

This marriage was solemnized by us William Warren Martin and (the mark of) Emily Barrett.'

"What does 'the mark of' mean'?" asked Kit.

"It means that Emily couldn't write her name and just signed the register with a mark, usually an X."

"So, that means William could write his name, and was probably educated before entering the workhouse."

"I should think so. I don't suppose children received much education in a workhouse. Maybe it means too, the boys hadn't been in the workhouse very long."

Kit beamed with pleasure then added, "Guess who the witnesses were?" Without waiting for a reply, she said, "His brother George Martin and a woman named Sarah Taylor." Excited now that she was in the right time period, Kit continued on, scrolling through the months of marriages.

"Got him," she announced triumphantly. "George Martin married Sarah Taylor in October of the same year, also in Barking."

"Well done. So that appears to be the connection to the Martins in the workhouse and, if they are the same Martins, their connection to Barking."

Kit couldn't wait to enter in the marriage details for the two brothers. "Now all I have to do is find the families on the census records."

Checking the Barking records for 1851 brought up the record for an Emily Martin, wife of a fisherman with two children. "Elizabeth Ann Martin age twenty, dressmaker, and Emily May age eighteen, lace maker. Emily herself is listed under occupation as a 'monthly nurse'."

"What's a monthly nurse?"

"I'm not sure," said Mike, "but we can look under Victorian occupations and see if it's listed."

Here, a 'monthly nurse' was someone who was hired to assist new mothers during the first month after their baby was born." He gave Kit a questioning glance. "That seems strange. I wonder if that required education or certification of some kind or could anyone hire themselves out? We know she couldn't read or write. Maybe you just had to have experience with children."

Kit made note of that on a separate notepad, intending to follow-up later. "I'm sure I'll find something on the internet about that profession."

"For now, I think I'll look for the 1841 census." It didn't take long for Kit to bring up the 1841 census for the Martin family.

"Here, William and Emily Martin. William age 45, a fisherman. Emily his wife also, age 45, and their children: Edward age twenty; William age 15, Joseph, age 15; Elizabeth Ann, age 10; Emily May, age 8; and a boarder named Thomas Webster, apprentice, age 15."

She looked at the census record thoughtfully. "Why are the ages in multiples of five?" she asked.

"That's the way they recorded the ages for the 1841 census, well most of the enumerators did. As to why, I don't know. Let me check." He entered the question into a search engine, scrolling down several sites until he found one that looked promising. "This says, those over 15 were rounded down to the nearest 5 years, so someone aged 43 would be recorded as 40, but children under 15 were usually recorded with their accurate age. Hmm, I wonder why?" He rephrased the question and came up with some more accurate responses. "Apparently the census was for a statistical purpose and the people organizing the information wanted to present the data in age groups of five-year increments. So, they grouped people 15-19, 20-24, 25-29 and so on. To save themselves time grouping the results they decided to have the enumerators do it for them. So, if you were 34, you'd be listed as 30, or if 18 you'd be listed as 15. So, most people were actually older than it showed. I guess if you wanted to be sure, you'd have to check the '51 census to check the more accurate ages." He smiled having found an answer to the question.

"I'm a little curious about the Thomas Webster. Maybe I'll see if I can find something more about him, or how he became an apprentice," said Mike.

After a few minutes of reading silently, Mike sighed. "I'm afraid your previous fears might apply in some cases. It's sad, but the life of an apprentice depended a lot upon the master he worked for. Some were treated as family members while others were considered basically slaves. Apparently, not all apprentices had a great life on the fishing boats, many were just a cheap commodity that were used until they died or were injured with no regard for their health or welfare. I suppose too, some might just 'disappear' overboard, so no one would know, if they were being abused. I found this article. It talked about the various apprentices that were beaten and starved, some so tortured that they died before returning home. It seemed the captains had ultimate control over them. Some captains were charged with wilful murder but few were convicted, even with eyewitness reports."

While Kit recorded her findings from the census records on the chart paper that was laid out on the dining room table, Mike read about a tragedy that resulted in a boy frozen to death in the north Atlantic near Iceland. "That's terrible," said Kit. "It sounds as if some of them were sadistic men, relishing in having someone to brutalize. I wonder how many were actually treated well."

"I found something." He waited for the next page to come up. "Look." It was a record of U.K. Apprentices Indentured in Merchant Navy, 1824 to 1910. '*August 1836. Thomas Webster, age when bound- 13. Date of indenture: August 27, 1836. Term for which bound: 8 years. Indenture expires: August 27 1844. Name and residence to whom bound: William Martin of Barking. Vessel in which Apprentice is to serve: Emma.*' Isn't that amazing! So, I guess that proves he was a fisherman?"

"I would say so. That's nice Thomas got to live with the family. It sounds as if he was treated better than the other boy you read about."

"I hope so. I would think all apprentices would live with or close to their masters, though, just to keep an eye on them. But then the fishing business was a brutal career choice with constant danger, and rough men."

"Wouldn't it be neat if he married one of the daughters," said Kit. "I'd like to follow up on the girls later and see who they married." She opened her notepad and jotted a reminder to follow-up on the children of William Martin and see what became of them.

The wall clock chimed and Mike suddenly became aware of the time. He double checked with the time on his watch. Five o'clock. "I'm sorry. I think I'll have to leave now. I have four framing jobs to get done for tomorrow morning before eleven."

Kit stood as Mike prepared his laptop to leave. "It's been a great day. Thanks for coming over."

He stopped, and looked at her. "It has, hasn't it. When shall we meet again, to do more work on William, I mean?" Kit could tell he suddenly felt flustered and tried to ease his discomfort.

She smiled. "I'm off at five tomorrow," she offered. "I have a meeting till ten on Tuesday then I have two weeks off. I'll probably get a start on the kitchen cabinets then."

"How is around five o'clock on Tuesday?" suggested Mike.

"Perfect, so I'll see you then."

She walked him to the door and watched as he backed up and drove away, looking forward very much to Tuesday afternoon.

The traffic was just as busy as Mike feared at the lunch time hour, but he'd been able to close shop and reach the Records Department just before noon. He found the building easily after speaking to a young clerk at city hall. Her parking advice and directions had helped him locate the appropriate department. He was surprised to find that the previous owner of the painting had been a widow. After paying a fee and waiting while the documents were found, Mike found himself reading the Last Will and Testament of, Lilian Northwood—her husband Ralph, having died two years before. It was a short Will with her lawyer as executor, no mention of any family and the whole of her estate left to the local Humane Society, once her belongings and property were sold and her debts paid. So, who was Edward Northwood? And was he actually a nephew of the Northwoods? And if he was, why was he left out of her Will? Could she have been unaware of her husband's nephew?

Folding the document and carefully enclosing it in the briefcase he'd brought, he nodded a farewell to the young lady who had retrieved the papers for him. He wondered what Kit was doing now. He glanced at the hall clock and thought she was probably having her lunch break. Should he call her and tell her what he'd done and what he'd found out or wait until he saw her tomorrow once he had more information. He'd know soon enough.

Mike had been nervous making the call; his hands shaking, hoping his voice wouldn't betray his intentions. Mr. Jenkins had answered in an impatient tone, obviously Mike had caught him at an inopportune time, yet he recovered quickly once Mike said he was calling for his fiancé Kit Morrison—a small deception he felt necessary to give his call some credence. With the pretence of reconsidering his offer, Perkins had been eager to have Mike speak with Mr. Northwood—most likely thinking of his hefty commission—and readily passed on the name of the hotel where Northwood was staying during his short stay in Canada.

He wasn't good at impromptu situations, so Mike rehearsed different scenarios in the car on the way to Elm Street Holiday Inn. Would he play it cautious and try to catch Northwood in a lie or just come out and say he didn't believe he was who he said he was? At the moment he didn't know.

The parking spots were along the side and continued to the back of the building. The lot was crowded with the comings and goings of travellers, many carrying suitcases either just arriving, or leaving. A car backed out of its place leaving a spot and Mike quickly pulled in and parked. He sat in his car, his nerves starting to play on his decision to pursue his plan. Should he mention Lilian Northwood's Will, or just ask why he was so interested in buying the painting? He checked his watch; he'd have to get back to the shop soon. No use sitting in the car thinking about what to do.

For a busy hotel, the front desk was surprisingly void of people. A tall thin man stood behind the counter watching the few guests as they moved about the reception area. A bellhop assisted an elderly couple with their luggage and Mike moved aside as he came through the glass doors to allow the young man room to manoeuvre the luggage cart he was pushing. The bellhop nodded his thanks as Mike made his way toward the front desk.

The clerk greeted him affably, and Mike felt his shoulders relax slightly only now realizing how tense he'd been. "I've come to see Mr. Edward Northwood," said Mike. "I believe he is a guest here."

The young man—Watson it said on his name tag— turned to check the in-box then as if suddenly realizing something, turned back to Mike. "Mr. Northwood has just checked out, I'm afraid." Then in an effort to be helpful, he added, "You probably passed him as he was leaving. Tall man with a black trench coat over his arm and a small black suitcase."

"Thank you. Maybe I can catch up to him." And before Mr. Watson could respond Mike was out through the glass doors and off at a jog toward the parking lot. He did remember seeing the man; standing beneath the roof-overhang as he lit up a cigarette. Mike searched the area focusing on single individuals, but then maybe Northwood had been waiting for a cab and was on his way to Kit's house now; Pat did say he'd stepped out of a cab when he approached her at the house, and she seemed to think he would return. Movement caught his eye. Towards the rear of the parking lot, he saw the man flick the remainder of his cigarette to the ground before getting into a black van. It was him. The vehicle started and Mike doubted he could have reached the van before it drove across the lot and out the far exit, but he could see it from where he stood and could also read the larger print of the business logo that ran along the side of the door—Scottlea Art Gallery, Mississauga.

He stood, stunned, his mind running over the numerous possibilities and dozens of more questions. Was Edward Northwood actually an employee of Scottlea Art Gallery Mississauga? How could he check this out? Or was Northwood just a friend of someone working at Scottlea and had borrowed their van? And why was the painting so important? Why had someone placed the clipping in the back of the painting? Were the Northwoods somehow related to the Barking fisherman? He had a lot to think about, the first was to check out the Scottlea Art Gallery.

Mike shook his head slowly; reality suddenly overtaking the adrenaline he'd experienced in the parking lot. Up until last week his life had been fairly routine and uneventful, boring if he were truthful. Now, he was playing amateur sleuth; albeit, one who had a beautiful partner. He smiled to himself thinking of her and couldn't wait to see Kit again. Tomorrow, at five.

It was late. Mike had returned to his shop shortly after two, and replaced the 'closed' side of the sign with the one that said 'open'. He'd had four customers during the rest of the afternoon which allowed him to finish up the orders he'd promised for the next morning.

By seven o'clock he'd finished for the day and now found himself sitting in his apartment at the kitchen table with his laptop before him entering in the information he'd discovered in the parking lot of the Holiday Inn.

He clicked on the Scottlea Art Gallery site, a Gallery which specialized in mid-nineteenth-century art, and waited for the page to appear. Along the top of the page, he found the 'about us' tab, which when opened showed the photographs of two men; Alistair Shelby, Administrator, and Frank T. Saulter, Director. He looked at the familiar face. It was him; Saulter was the man with the cigarette under the Holiday Inn awning. Edward Northwood was an imposter.

So, Frank Saulter was an art conservator and art dealer, but why would he want an unsigned painting of a Barking harbour and go to such lengths to get it? What did he know?

Even more puzzling—How did he know about the painting?

Chapter 6

The upper cabinet shells on one wall had been lightly sanded, primed by noon, and now stood gleaming with their final melamine coat of white. Kit stood back, admiring her work. The white gave a clean look to the room compared to the original faded walnut-stained wood. Her father would have chided her for covering up any wood surface with paint and would have even offered to help her sand them down fully to the bare wood and re-stain them. But the kitchen was small and she liked the idea of a bright room; the white would hopefully accomplish that.

The door bell rang which startled her; she still wasn't use to Beethoven's Fifth being played out in such vibrancy above the kitchen door. There were ways to change the tune but she hadn't bothered to figure that out yet, maybe today would be the day. She glanced at the kitchen clock: five-twenty—Mike. Realizing she had forgotten about the time; thoroughly engrossed in her work, she set the brush she'd been using down on the rim of the paint can, and hurried to the door.

He stood there grinning at her, holding his usual satchel containing his laptop as well as several newspaper-wrapped smaller packages. The scent of fish and chips wafted from the door and her stomach also noticing the enticing smell, gave a sound of approval.

"I figured you might not have time to think about supper yet, so I took the liberty." He smiled at the oversized shirt she was wearing, originally navy blue, now splotched with white drips and smudges where she

58

had wiped her hands. Strands of hair, having escaped from their clip hung in curls, framing her face.

"I'm very glad you did because I worked through lunch, too. Thank you, it smells delicious." Kit took two of the packages handed to her while Mike hung up his jacket.

"Come on, we'll eat at the kitchen bar, then you can see my handiwork."

Once in the kitchen, Kit took out cutlery and two plates from an open cupboard, one she hadn't got to yet with her white melamine paint.

Mike sat at the bar, while Kit took one of the stools and slid it to the other side so she could face Mike.

Mike glanced at the finished cabinet, as he passed Kit one of the fish dinners; a small box full of fries with a deep-fried piece of battered fish resting across the top.

"The paint job looks great," he said sincerely. "What a difference from the dark wood colour; it absolutely brightens up the room."

Kit turned to look at the finished side of the room. "I'm pleased with it." She emptied the contents of her box onto her plate. "Haven't quite decided yet whether to paint the doors white or use an accent colour." She picked up a fry, considering. "Maybe Pat will have a better idea."

"Ketchup or vinegar?" she asked.

"Vinegar, please." Kit went to the cabinet that held the oil and vinegar.

"I haven't had fish and chips from an actual fish and chip shop for years." She closed her eyes in bliss, just now realizing how hungry she'd been.

Mike squirted some vinegar on his fries. "Me too, I skipped lunch trying to finish up some orders and thought this would hit the spot."

She smiled as he added some vinegar to his fish as well, while she chose ketchup for her fries.

"Oh, I didn't get a chance to tell you," she said, giving him a slight smile indicating a secret. "After you left Sunday, I suddenly remembered I had someone who lived in London that might be able to help us. I have a second cousin, at least I think she's my second cousin." She stopped to consider. "Maybe she's once removed, although I'm not sure exactly what that means, anyway; she's my mother's cousin's daughter. Her name is Jennet." Mike sat back, a piece of battered fish dangling from his fork, waiting for the importance of this story to emerge. "I met her when my mother and I went to London three years ago. Jennet lives in Chiswick. We write occasionally; so, Sunday, I emailed her after you left and asked her if she could go to Kew, it's not too far away, and look up William Warren Martin and see what she might find. I gave her the information that we thought might be his." Kit smiled triumphantly after finishing her story.

"Great idea. There are a lot of records at Kew that aren't on the internet." Kew which held a combination of Public Records and Historical documents was open for researchers to go and look through their records.

He continued with his meal, and smiled in satisfaction; glad now that he had thought to bring supper. "Well, I have an important discovery to share with you."

"Oh, what is this great revelation you've made?"

The sun came through the kitchen window giving his face a slight flushed glow. "Well, first I went to city hall and got a copy of the Northwood Will. I didn't realize that it was Mrs. Northwood who had recently died, although unless both her and her husband had died in a car accident, it stands to reason that there would just be one of them left. Anyway, in her Will she left everything to the local Humane Society. Not one mention of an Edward Northwood. Then, I posed as your fiancé," he paused as his face took on a slightly darker shade of pink, as he looked down avoiding her eyes, "and got the name of the hotel where Edward Northwood was staying, from Perkins. I tracked him down in the parking lot and found out he was actually an art dealer in Mississauga and his name is Frank Saulter not Northwood."

Kit looked at him in disbelief, totally missing the important part of his discovery. "You posed as my fiancé?"

Mike gave her a sheepish look, a french fry left impaled on his fork in mid-air. "Well just for a minute, when I spoke to Perkins. I needed some pretence for calling him." Then he smiled, pleased with himself. "But it worked, he was more than eager to give me the information once I suggested you might be interested in his proposition." He ate the suspended potato and nodded toward her plate suggesting she eat before her food got cold.

"Don't you see. Saulter found out Lily Northwood had this painting. How, and why he wants it is the mystery." He frowned, suddenly in thought. "I wonder if the fisherman has anything to do with this or …" His train of thought lost, he shrugged. "Maybe we'll find out if we keep looking for more about William Martin."

Calmed now over his deception, Kit considered this. "I don't suppose we could call Saulter up and ask him."

He laughed. "Probably not. At least if he tries to contact you again, we will be more prepared to talk to him."

"We?"

"Well … yes," he replied, a bit affronted. "I kind of thought we were pursuing this hunt and wherever it led, together."

"Yes, you're right. And I appreciate your efforts so far, and I do wish to continue looking for William Martin with you. Let's hope your Saulter doesn't call again." Kit smiled. "Let's finish supper and go back to our research." She looked at the small splatter of white paint on her hand. "Besides, I need a break from painting."

She watched as Mike finished his meal, while she enjoyed hers and was glad he was here. She was surprised he had gone to so much trouble to find Edward Northwood, now known as Saulter and wondered what he would have done if he'd been confronted by the man at the hotel. There was a lot to think about, but for now, they would work together and worry about Saulter when the time came.

◆ ◆ ◆

Kit opened up her laptop and scanned the screen, as Mike prepared his computer for their research.

"I just saw that I have mail. I haven't been on the computer since Sunday. There's an email from Jennet."

Mike pulled his chair back and went to see what Kit had found. She was on her email site, ready to open the email that had arrived mid-afternoon. Mike pulled up the spare chair on Kit's side of the table and gave her arm a squeeze in anticipation. They watched as a letter from her cousin appeared.

'Dear Kit. So nice to hear from you. It's been a while, since we've chatted on line. Mum says 'hello' too, and hopes all is well with you and your family. You seemed to have discovered an interesting story. I was able to go to Kew on Monday. I only had less than an hour during my break, but I did find something that seemed to match your guy. Let me know if this is of any help to you. I won't get a chance to go again until the end of the week, as I will be away for a few days in the north. Cheers, Jennet.'

"I'm so glad I thought of contacting Jennet. I don't know her that well, having just met her the once but we hit it off and have been keeping in touch ever since. It was so good of her to go and look up the name for us."

"Oh, wow." He looked at the attachment that came with the email, a photocopy of the documents she had found—Register of Seamen's Tickets. William Martin born in Dartford, appeared to be in the Merchant Marine. The document was from 1845 and gave his age as 53. The record gave a physical description of the man as well. "How amazing to know what he actually looked like." Height—five feet, six inches tall. Complexion—

fair. Hair—dark brown. Eyes—hazel. Marks—scar on left cheek. "It also asks when he first went to sea."

"He went to sea as an apprentice in the year 1802," read Kit. "When unemployed, he resided at Barking. So, does that mean he went from the workhouse to apprentice?"

"It might be," said Mike. "What was the date you have for his birth?"

"1792."

"It fits."

"I thought he was a fisherman. How come he's in the Merchant Marine?"

"I don't know. Maybe he became a fisherman later in life. There's forty years between the workhouse and the 1841 census."

"Maybe, but this shows he was in the Merchant Marine after the '41 census."

Kit looked at the results she had started to enter, before them. "I know most of this has to be positively proven, but I think we are on the right trail. We have a birth in Dartford, with a brother. We have the same names in a workhouse as children. I have found both marriages in Barking and we have him on an 1851 and 1841 census. And, of course, if it's the same man, we know about his death."

Mike studied the information Kit had written on the cartridge paper. "When I got home last night, I thought we might need a genealogy site that had access to old newspapers in the London and surrounding areas, so I took out a trial subscription to two family history websites that had both records and newspapers."

"That's great. Maybe we'll find out more about William's death and see if there was a trial for the man who murdered him. The clipping did say an inquest was to follow. Maybe there's a newspaper story about that."

"Here." Mike passed her the name of the sites and his password.

He was glad now that he had gone ahead and furthered their record availability, eager as Kit was to find out more.

Engrossed in the pages they were discovering, each worked, focused, until Mike broke the silence. "I searched for the 'British Merchant Marine records 1845' and found a site that should explain the record Jennet found." Kit paused her reading and listened. She smiled at Mike's enthusiasm and was glad she had someone working with her that knew how to find information on the internet.

"This article says from 1835 on, the British government wanted to keep track of all seamen including fishermen, in case there was a sudden need for men in the Navy or Merchant Marine during a time of war. So, anyone who sailed for a living including fishermen were registered and given a ticket number and records of their trips were kept. Our guy was probably a fisherman and that explains why he was on this list. Maybe we will be able to find records of some of the fishing trips he made."

"That is interesting. I don't know much about British history, but I wonder if any of them had to go to war? Maybe the Crimean War?"

"That would be interesting to research. I'm going to try looking here."

Mike opened a new window and typed in the 'British Archives'. There was a lengthy section on the Merchant Marines. Once finding the information he was looking for, the site directed him to another genealogy site that held those records, obviously affiliated with the Archives. "We're in luck," said Mike. "This is one of the sites we can use." He typed in the name and dates then waited to see what came up. "Here, under Britain, Merchant Seamen, 1835-1857, is a list of men and their ticket number." The page showed the name of the seaman, his ticket number and where he was born. "What were the names of his eldest sons?"

Kit flipped through her notes, "Um…Edward, William and Joseph."

"Look, here," he said, excited that he may have found the family. "William Martin born Dartford, ticket number 3306, and George Martin born Dartford, number 3389. Then if you look down there are the names, albeit, there are a few names the same but this Edward, William and Joseph are all born in Barking and notice the ticket numbers, they are much larger and close to each other in sequence. We can't prove it, although the census records might show, but it seems his sons joined him in the fishing business."

"That's amazing. Can you print that out, or save it?"

Pleased with his results, Mike saved the page to his laptop. He went back to the previous page intending to look at the other search results that had come up.

"There are probably more records at Kew I could ask Jennet to—"

Beethoven's Fifth announced a visitor.

Kit left the table and quickly went to answer the door. A tall man, standing under the glow of her outside-door light, smiled affably. With their concentration focused on their work she hadn't realized it was getting dark outside. "Hello, may I speak with Kit Morrison?"

The voice was pleasant and definitely British. Knowing he was an imposter, Kit wondered which British actor he had spent time copying. "I'm Kit, won't you come in." She made room for him as he stepped into the small foyer. Curious, Mike joined her. He smiled at Frank Saulter and introduced himself. Saulter smiled and turned back to Kit. "I am Edward Northwood. Mr. Perkins informed me that possibly you might have changed your mind about the picture after speaking with your fiancé." He gave Mike a questioning glance.

"Um, yes, I see," said Kit, with a side smirk at Mike. "I'm afraid you've made a trip for nothing Mr. Northwood. As I told Mr. Perkins—she waved a hand toward the painting which he couldn't see from the doorway into the living room—I'm quite pleased with the painting and don't wish to sell it."

His brow creased slightly contemplating. "What if I made a final offer of one thousand dollars. I would really like to have it."

"That is a very generous offer Mr. Northwood, but I must say no, I'm sorry."

His eyes hardened at that, and his face lost its initial friendly expression. "Very well then. Thank you for your time." With that he turned and left, walking back to the taxi that had been told to wait for him along the side of the road.

Kit closed the door as Saulter opened the door of the cab, then she locked it, her hand shaking as it left the latch.

She gave Mike a blank look. "You're right. There's something about that painting." Then she laughed softly. "You know, I was almost tempted to let him know we knew he was an imposter, and ask him why he wanted it so much."

Mike took her hands in his. She was still shaking, then he surrounded her with his arms, drew her close and hugged her until she stopped. "Better?"

"Yes. I'm so glad you were here." She released her arms and looked up him then smiled.

He tilted her head up just enough, then leaned in and kissed her, softly and firmly. "So am I."

She sighed. "What do we do now?"

He took her hand as they walked back to the dining room, turning on the living room lamp as they went. They stopped in front of the painting, and he kissed her once more.

"I'm not sure. I know someone who works at a Niagara art gallery. Maybe I could call and ask him for his opinion."

She nodded in agreement. "That sounds like a good idea."

"But until then we can just keep looking for William Martin." Mike glanced at the wall clock. "It's getting late. I have to work until twelve tomorrow, then I'm off until Monday."

◆ ◆ ◆

He smiled, thinking of the knowing look on his sister's face as he had explained what he and Kit were doing. He'd told her about the Saulter connection and after a few questions regarding his safety, she had agreed to mind the store for the next four days, providing she could bring her young child with her.

"Do you like this girl?" she had asked. At first, he hadn't known what to say, and after a look from his older sister, had finally confessed that he did.

"I enjoy her company; we get along great." Then awkwardly he had added, "I want to get to know her better."

◆ ◆ ◆

"Come for lunch," Kit said, "then we can work together for a while." At Mike's raised eyebrow, she added, "Yes, I do have food."

He laughed. "Okay, see you at noon."

Chapter 7

Kit sat at the living room window waiting for Mike to arrive. She'd had a restless night; meeting Frank Saulter had unnerved her, and Mike's kiss had had a similar, yet opposite effect. She wondered if that was the last they would hear from Saulter, and she wondered how far her relationship with Mike would go. By nine, she'd had only four hours sleep and now sat looking out the window waiting.

He was punctual and pulled into her driveway, just as Pat arrived and parked along the side of the road. Kit waved as he approached the door, then waited and held it open as Pat stepped through carrying an armload of fabric samples.

"Thanks, I brought these for you to look at," Pat said. "I'd really love your opinion."

"You look as though you've been busy."

"Busy is not the word for it. More like, run ragged."

"I'm just about to make lunch, have you eaten?"

"No, and I'd love to join you … two." She glanced at Mike who was setting up his machine in the dining room, then gave Kit a knowing look. "Looks like things are progressing."

Kit responded with a small smile. "I think so." Then amending her answer, she added, "Oh, you mean Mike." Then laughed. "Come on, we'll fill you in over burgers."

❖ ❖ ❖

"I didn't think he'd have the nerve to come back. Do you think he will try to get the painting again, maybe offer more for it?" suggested Pat.

"I don't think so," said Mike. "He knows for sure Kit won't sell it; so, short of breaking in and stealing it, there's not much more he can do."

Kit set the salad bowl down between them. "I'll get the burgers," said Mike, and left the two at the kitchen counter while he checked the meat on the bar-b-que.

"I wonder what's so special about that painting?" pondered Pat. "Maybe there's an espionage micro-chip embedded it in some how. You know, with a list of spies, or even a secret map to a treasure."

Kit laughed at these scenarios. "Boy, you have been working hard. You're becoming delusional." She took the buns out of the toaster oven as Mike rejoined them.

"Why don't you and I look at the samples you brought after lunch, while Mike works on the computer."

❖ ❖ ❖

"I need something to go with this pale sage," said Pat. The fabric samples were laid out across the back of the couch and across the floor of the back room so the girls could stand back and see them from a distance.

"I like this one," said Kit. The leaf print has both the pale sage and a darker one. And the cream background is neutral. You said she had a cat too, so this tight weave will last longer if it decides to scratch the couch."

"You're right. And it will go with her copper accents." Pat held up her choice for the family room. "What do you think of this?"

"I like the feel of the corduroy fabric." Kit looked again at the photo Pat had taken of the family room fireplace. "And it goes great with the brick on the fireplace wall."

It was almost an hour later when Kit and Pat heard a triumphant shout from the dining room. "I found something," he called.

The girls rushed in to find Mike grinning from ear to ear, just waiting to reveal his discovery.

Kit stood behind him, her arms resting on his shoulders hoping to see the screen with its results, but the window had been closed. "What did you find?"

Enjoying the drama, Mike began by telling how he had been searching for trials in the nineteenth-century and had come upon a site called Old Baily. It had the 'Proceedings of the Old Baily from 1674 – 1913'. It had the actual documents of the trials with the witnesses, the attorney's questioning and the sentencing. Old Baily adjoined Newgate Prison and, by the mid 1800s, heard serious crimes from across England, not just the London and Middlesex areas.

"Look, here's one dated 1859,"—his explanation done, he brought up the window with the information—"the trial of Albert Burridge."

Mike read the page's introduction of the trial. '*Albert Burridge was indicted for feloniously assaulting William Warren Martin on February 18th wounding him with the intent of theft. 2nd count- stating his intent to be, to do him some grievous bodily harm.*'

He then brought up the trial proceeds for the girls to read.

'Mr. Harrison conducted the prosecution.

Sarah Coleman: I am the wife of Jacob Coleman. I live at 30 Axe Street Barking. I was outside attending to my garden. I was expecting Mr. Martin to bring a picture he was painting. My husband had commissioned his work. My attention was attracted by a man who carried a long piece of lumber. He approached Mr. Martin and hit him across the head. He then took the painting that had fallen to the ground and destroyed it by stepping through the canvas. I saw no other blow struck. I went to help Mr. Martin after Albert Burridge fled the scene and stayed with him until the police came.

Question from the court: Do you see that man in court now?

Sarah Coleman: Yes, He is the prisoner, Albert Burridge.

Samuel Denton: My name is Samuel Denton. I sell poultry. I went to the Copper Arms just before eight o'clock on the 18th. While there, I saw the prisoner with four others. He was intoxicated. Mr. Martin came in shortly after, where upon Burridge began taunting him. He accused him of cheating him.

Michael Struthers: My name is Michael Struthers. I live at 23 Fulton Street. I am a surgeon. I saw the injured man that evening after he had been attacked. He had a gash on his forehead and seemed confused. He was bleeding from the wound.

Charles Wheaton: My name is Charles Wheaton. I work with William Martin on his fishing boat Emma. I am a fisherman.

73

Question from the Court: Do you know the prisoner?

Charles Wheaton: Yes. He is also a fisherman. He had accused William Martin of interfering with his fishing nets. Which I must say is not true.

John O'Leary (police-constable G 48.): I went into the Copper Arms, and found Burridge there—I took the prisoner into custody—he resisted violently—kicking me several times on the legs, he put his leg between mine, and attempted to throw me down.

Albert Burridge- guilty of assault and theft- three years imprisonment'

"Wow, it does seem to appear to be our William Martin, doesn't it?" said Kit, amazed that such records still existed.

Having read the transcript through for the third time Mike was now connecting the dots. "Kit! Our man was also a painter!"

"My painting. Could he really have painted it?"

"We didn't see a signature," said Pat.

"No, but maybe we just missed it," offered Kit.

Mike pushed his chair away from the table. "Maybe. Why don't we look at it closer."

◆ ◆ ◆

Once Mike had the picture off the wall, he placed it on a towel that Kit had laid out on the coffee table to protect it.

"Look somewhere along the left or right-hand corner. That's the usual place where artists signed their work."

Kit turned on all the lights in the living room to better see the painting under different light angles.

"I don't know," said Pat. "It doesn't look like there is anything there."

"Kit, do you have a magnifying glass?" asked Mike.

"I do, but I'm not sure where it is, I still have boxes to unpack. I'll check the cabinet drawer." Kit left them and went into the back room to check her cabinet that usually held most of her stationary needs, returning with a large circular magnifying glass.

Handing it to Mike she sat on the couch opposite, with Pat sitting next to her.

"Here, look, I think this is a number." Mike handed the glass to Kit inviting her to look.

"Yes, 48. He's painted it almost the same colour as the pier."

"Can you see a name?"

"No, but there are some marks just before it."

Mike joined her and together they looked for some reference to a name.

"There, it looks like two X's, touching." Mike pointed to the spot where he could make out a different colour of paint forming the letters.

"That doesn't make any sense," said Pat. "Why wouldn't he just write his name?" Then added, "Unless he couldn't read or write, and signed with an X."

"He could write," said Kit. "He signed his name on his marriage certificate in 1820."

Mike looked at the letters again through the magnifying glass. "Maybe they're just marks on the stone pier, not letters at all," then reconsidered, "but they are in line with the date and they're the same size."

"But they're not separate letters," noticed Kit. "They're carefully joined at the edges."

Kit went to the dining room and returned with a pen and piece of paper. She sat back on the couch next to Pat and drew the two X's next to a 48.

"Try making them larger," suggested Pat.

Kit drew them again, making them larger and edges touching. Suddenly Pat gasped. "I think I have it. What are his initials?"

"William Martin, so W and M," said Mike.

"Well, don't you see it. It's his initials."

Mike came over to sit next to Kit while Pat took the paper and drew a large W. Then just below it she drew a widened M making sure the top of the M touched the bottom of the W; so that they were a mirror image of each other.

"Oh, my gosh, you're right," said Mike. "It has to be. Well, figures it would take a decorator to notice a detail like that. Well done, Pat."

Pat gave a slight bow and prepared to leave. "Glad to be of help, but I have to be going now. I have an appointment with a painter at four." Then she chuckled at the small joke she had made. "Thanks for your help with the fabric, Kit. It's nice to have some validation. Have fun searching."

Kit and Mike were suddenly alone with this revelation and still sat in the living room in disbelief, contemplating what this meant. It appeared that the fisherman in the asylum had been a painter as well, twenty years earlier.

But the question remained; why did Saulter want the picture? What did he know?

Mike leaned back on the couch. "I don't know about you but I'm ready to relax a bit. This has been most stressful. Great, but stressful." He smiled. "So, what shall it be: paint cabinets or go fishing?"

Kit took his hand in hers and kissed him on the cheek. "Well, fishing of course."

"Good, I came prepared with my brother-in-law's fishing rods."

◆ ◆ ◆

They took the car this time and parked at the opposite end of the bridge they had crossed a few days earlier, in the small area reserved for visitors. Mike opened the trunk and retrieved the fishing rods and a small box of lures. They walked hand-in-hand down the sloping discarded road that used to divide the pond into two areas, careful of the faded jagged asphalt of decades gone by. The sound of crickets and frogs could be heard as they approached the pond. Grasshoppers hopped away as the grass they were on was disturbed by their feet.

The sun was out and the day had become warmer as it approached mid-afternoon. The grandfather and boy they had encountered before were not there, so Kit and Mike walked down past the edge of the bridge to the same spot they had seen them fishing from.

The air was still, with a hint of humidity, and the pond was smooth and shimmering.

Mike separated the rods and straightened out the lines, adding a small lure to each. "I never thought to ask, have you fished before?"

Kit laughed. "Several years ago, yes." Then taking the rod Mike offered her, she took a casting stance. "Okay, where do you want the lure to land."

Taking up the challenge, he surveyed the area. "There,"—he pointed to a small island of growth to their right— "just in front of that grassy patch of ground." He stood back as Kit cast her line, landing the lure just in front of the target hillock. She started to reel in the line, triumphant.

"Nice," was all Mike could say, suitably impressed, then prepared his own line. "There are a lot of frogs here," he said. "I think I'll try a small rubber frog instead." He picked up a small green frog, it legs wobbling as he attached it to his line, and cast out to the left of Kit's lure.

He gave the lure a bit of action as he reeled it in, stopping every so often to allow the legs to straighten then flex forward as the frog was pulled again. Kit laughed at the action of the lure and noticed he seemed to enjoy working the frog as it swam across the water and wondered if he'd actually care whether he caught a fish or not.

They spent most of the next hour casting and reeling in their lures with no success at tempting a fish—if there were any fish in this part of the pond.

There were benches along the paths to the pond where the two now sat enjoying the sights and sounds of the pond, shaded by the surrounding trees.

"This is nice," said Mike. "You can hear all the sounds clearly. The bees, the birds—. Look, over there at the edge of the island." He pointed toward a spot on the island, close to where they had been casting. "I think it's a heron. I've seen larger blue herons, but not this smaller variety before. The bird moved ever so slightly then froze, watching. Without warning it plunged its long beak into the water and snatched a frog from the grassy edge. "I'm glad he didn't try that with my lure, we both would have had a surprise."

Kit leaned against his shoulder. She was enjoying this moment, being here with Mike. She was noticing more about him the more they spent time together. She found him to be intelligent, good natured, kind, and very attractive.

A fluttering movement on a flowering shrub across from them caught her eye. An orange butterfly had stumbled into an orb-weaving spider's web and was helplessly trying to escape. "Look."

Mike followed her gaze then watched as Kit went over to free the captive. She gently removed the web from the butterfly's feet as it rested on her finger, then set it on another shrub, watching it as it moved its wings experimentally. After a moment it flew off.

"There's your good deed for the day."

"I'm sure the spider wouldn't think so." She sat down by Mike again watching the butterfly as it fluttered around the vegetation surrounding their bench. "How was your morning?"

"A bit hurried," said Mike. "I did have one neat piece to frame up. It was a rubbing, done in a gold-copper colour."

"A rubbing?"

"Yes, the client had been to London at a Brass Rubbing centre where they had brass replicas of real brass portraits of medieval knights and ladies that had been placed on the burial vault. They use replicas now because the originals are protected. Anyway, they let people come and place a paper over the brass picture and rub it with a coloured wax crayon. This rubbing was done in gold crayon on black paper. It was quite striking once the frame was on."

"Brass rubbings are a hobby for many people. This one wasn't to scale, but was just as nice." Mike fished out his cellphone from his jeans pocket and found the last picture he had taken that morning. "Here, I took a picture of it, before the owner picked it up."

Kit adjusted the screen position to reduce the glare of the sun and saw a beautifully framed picture of a knight, holding his sword and shield. "That's amazing. I bet it took a while to carve the original. Look at all the detail. The gold frame is perfect too."

The sudden discussion of framing brought back the thought of her painting. "What do you think we should do about my picture?" The thought of Saulter coming to her home still had an unnerving effect.

"I think we should have it looked at by someone at a gallery. I met a guy last year at a trade show. We had lunch together and we got on well. He works in the

Falls. Maybe he could shed some light on the picture for us, give us an idea if it's worth anything."

The sound of feet echoing on the metal bridge interrupted his thought. The old man and his grandson had arrived at the pond, fishing rods in hand. The man waved as he recognized the young couple sitting on the bench near the edge of the pond where they had been a few days before. "Any luck?" he called.

"No," said Mike. "Just a lot of casting practice."

The old man laughed. "You're not using the right kind of bait."

Kit and Mike watched as the two new fishermen walked to the end of the bridge then climbed down the slope to the spot where they were sitting below. The man took off his Tilley hat and wiped his forehead with the back of his hand. "A little too humid a day for my liking," he admitted, "but I suppose any day is good for fishing."

He opened up a plastic bag he carried attached to his belt. "These, work best for the fish here," he said, and reached in and took out a few coloured mini-marshmallows. "They work even better if you let them sit in garlic powder for a while."

Kit could smell the garlic powder from where she sat. "Thanks, we'll have to remember that for next time," she said.

Mike stood up to look at the small objects held out for him to see. "Really, is that all you use?"

The boy had run over to the edge of the pond eager to get started, and called to his grandfather.

"Usually," said the man. "Carp and catfish seem to find them intriguing." He waved at the boy. "I better go."

Kit joined Mike as the man put the marshmallows back into is bag. "Enjoy your fishing," she said in farewell. "Maybe we'll see you here again. Bye."

They walked hand-in-hand up the worn neglected asphalt road to their car, glad that they didn't have to walk back in the heat of the day.

Chapter 8

"Liam McQuarrie, please." Mike waited as the receptionist connected him with the office of Liam McQuarrie, art dealer and archivist. He smiled at Kit as he waited, listening to the recording asking for him to leave a message. "Hi, Liam. It's Mike Reynolds, we met last summer at the trade show. If you have time, I have a painting I would like your opinion on." Mike gave Kit's phone number as contact number, knowing she'd be home for the next few days, if he had time to see it.

"There, done. I hope he has time to speak to us."

"Shall we work on the research a bit more?" asked Kit.

"We could, or we could have some supper first."

Kit checked the clock. "It's a little early but by the time I get things ready it should be closer to six. How does 'lasagne and salad' sound?"

"That sounds great. Why don't I work some more until it's ready?"

Leaving Mike in the dining room, Kit went into the kitchen to prepare the salad while the lasagne heated up in the oven.

About fifteen minutes later, Kit joined Mike at his computer. "Have you found out any more about our fisherman?"

"Yes." He was focused on the site he was on, then smiled. "Something interesting, just waiting for this page. Here, William Martin, born 1792, occupation fisherman, was admitted to the West Ham workhouse infirmary on Saturday, February 19th 1859. He was discharged February 25, 1859."

"Looks like Burridge got his wish. Seems it was more than just a bad bump on the head."

"I did find one other piece of important information," offered Mike. It was on a new site that Mike had found the admission records for Creighton Lee Asylum. "I found him, under the 'UK. Lunacy Patient Admission Register, 1846-1912'. William Martin admitted May 3, 1859. Then it shows when he left the asylum." There was only one entry; April 23 1868, written under the column of deceased.

"He was there almost ten years then. I wonder if the attack by Burridge affected him mentally," suggested Kit. "Maybe that's why he was placed in an asylum. His brain was damaged."

"That might be so. I'm not sure how we can be sure, unless it says in the asylum records where he was killed. They may have something further at Kew that isn't online."

"Good idea, I'll update Jennet with the information we have now and ask her to check next time she goes, for anything new."

❖ ❖ ❖

A creaking hinge of a door opening brought her out of the pre-haze sleep that had finally absorbed her around two o'clock in the morning. Kit lay still, not sure she had actually heard something or not. Her bedroom opened up to a smaller room that she used as a study which had access to the living room below by a metal spiral staircase. There was an outdoor balcony off that room that overlooked the front yard garden. She listened, not moving. Then heard a sound below.

Her night table had a small flashlight in the drawer meant for emergencies should the power go out. She kept her light off and reached into the drawer, groping for the aluminium case of the small light. Her room was mildly lit from the street light outside her home. It gave enough light for her to walk to the study.

She heard a noise that sounded like someone moving things in the room below. She felt her heart race, then decided to confront the intruder.

She went to the staircase and peered down and saw a shadowy figure near the fireplace. She turned on her flashlight and pointed it down into the room below. "Who's there?" she called. There was a sound of scuffling and a closing of a door. "Someone's down stairs," she called to an imaginary person. Whoever it had been, had fled. The painting which she could see above the fireplace was tilted but still there. He must have been after the painting. Her hand started to shake with the after effects of almost being robbed. She opened the balcony door just in time to see a dark figure run down the street. There was the whine of a car starting up and the sound of it as it left. She ran back to her bedroom and grabbed her cellphone.

"Mike. It's Kit," she whispered. "Someone, was just in my house. I think he was after the painting. Thank you. Yes. Okay. I'll wait at the front."

It took Mike just ten minutes to arrive. When he did, he found Kit sitting in the dark on the top deck of her home, quite unnerved. She stood by the railing as he got out of his car.

"Are you all right? Are you hurt at all?" he called quietly, not wanting to wake the neighbours.

"No, I'm fine. Just a little shaken. I'll come down."

"No. Wait until I check around the house first." She nodded and sat down again to wait.

After a few minutes, Mike returned. "It's all right, he's gone. I'll wait by the front door."

Her eyes suddenly welled with emotion, as she opened the front door and hugged him with all the intensity of a drowning victim who had just been saved.

"I'm so glad you're here."

They stood in front of the fireplace looking up at the painting. The kitchen window had been forced and whoever it was had come in that way then opened up the sliding patio doors to the sunroom and unlocked the back door.

Mike sat on the couch with Kit laying sideways, her head on a pillow in his lap. His hand soothingly brushing back her hair, calming her.

"I should probably call the police," she said quietly.

"Probably. But what could they do. The burglar was frightened off and didn't appear to steal anything. You didn't see him or the car. If he was a pro, he probably wore gloves; so, no fingerprints, if indeed the cops bother to look for any."

She repositioned her legs against the end of the couch; trying to get comfortable. "I guess you're right, besides what could we say? That we think Saulter hired someone to steal the painting. We'd have to give some proof as to why it's worth stealing."

"True, but then again," said Mike, reconsidering, "if there is another break-in, it would be good to have proof of the previous one. I think you should call them, at least have a report filed."

"Yes, I suppose you're right. I better call now."

❖ ❖ ❖

"Miss Kit Morrison?" He was tall, and sun-tanned, with a thin mustache and looked very authoritative. He stood by the door with notebook in hand as Kit invited him in. Mike after being introduced, stood back a bit allowing Kit to explain the events of the last few hours. A small pang of jealously hit, as the officer, who seemed about their age, took a concerned interest in Kit.

After checking the forced window and making specific notes of the painting as Kit explained the thief was attempting to remove, Officer Anders confirmed that there wasn't a lot they could do, but at least there'd be an official report. He smiled pleasantly as he left and—which Mike thought rather unorthodox—gave her his card with his number which she could call if another break-in occurred.

Kit watched as the patrol car left and then bolted the door. "He was very nice, but as you thought, nothing much will be done."

Mike stood behind her and gave her a warm embrace.

"It's late," he said. "I'll stay here. You go back to bed and try not to worry. I don't think the thief will try it again."

87

"Okay, I'll get a pillow and a blanket for you. Thanks, Mike."

He looked thoughtfully at the picture. "It's a good thing we hung it again with two screws. It made it more difficult to take down."

Kit chuckled at that. "He seemed a bit short to reach up that high. Too bad he hadn't thought to bring a stepladder."

"And if he does try it again, I'll call you for help." Then he laughed, glad now that they had involved the police and that her mood had turned from fear to thoughts of sleep.

◆ ◆ ◆

"Coffee?"

Kit sat down across from Mike. He'd woken earlier and was now preparing them both a cup of coffee.

"Did you get some sleep?" asked Mike.

"Around four o'clock, I think"—she checked the time on the microwave— "so maybe six hours." She yawned. "Thanks for staying over. If you hadn't been here, I would have been listening all night for the sound of doors opening."

"I'm glad we spoke to the police," said Mike. He smiled thinking of Officer Anders. "Although they could have sent an older, more experienced officer, or a woman." He gave Kit a sideways smile. Then a thought occurred to him; maybe the thief would come back. "I could take the painting to my shop if you think they might try again?"

"That's—"

The phone rang. Kit left her chair to answer it wondering who it might be. Maybe Pat calling for some help with her decorating.

"Hello? Yes, just a minute." She turned and held out the phone for Mike. "It's Liam McQuarrie."

"Hi, Liam." He smiled at Kit as McQuarrie explained he was available. "Yes, I'm here now. Great. 75 Main Street. See you soon."

Mike handed the phone back to Kit. "He seemed pleased that I had called him and is interested in looking at the painting. He's coming over now."

Liam McQuarrie wasn't what Kit had expected. He was short, thin and in his late sixties, with wispy white hair and piercing blue eyes, and he looked more like a mad scientist than an art connoisseur. He was charming and took his time at examining the painting which Mike had taken down and brought into the kitchen where the lighting was better.

"Very nice," said Liam. "And you're right, this does seem to be a signature, but not one I've seen before." He stepped back from the painting. "It is well done. And you say the artist was a fisherman?"

"Yes. But there is something else I didn't mention before," said Mike. "An art gallery director has been trying to buy the painting from Kit. He's been very persistent about it, offering as much as a thousand dollars."

"That is curious. A painting like this might get a hundred dollars at most," said McQuarrie.

Then Mike added, "He's also been posing as a family member of the painting's former owner to do so."

That piqued McQuarrie's interest and his brows furrowed as he considered this. "You mean he didn't approach you as a gallery employee?"

"No." Mike debated telling him more and decided after a glance at Kit, and her slight nod, that he would tell him everything they knew. "I did discover later that his name is Frank T. Saulter and he works in Mississauga. And last night someone broke into Kit's house and tried to steal the picture."

"I wonder …" He took out a notepad and jotted down the particulars of Frank T. Saulter. "Would it be possible to take this painting to our gallery and x-ray it. That might tell us more about why Mr. Saulter is so interested in this work."

Mike looked at Kit. It was her painting, it had to be her decision. "Of course," she said. "We'd both like to know if there is anything special about it. We've invested several hours in researching the artist."

"Very good. I'll call you in a few days." Once the painting was wrapped in a protective blanket and safely placed in McQuarrie's vehicle, he left with the promise to be in touch as soon as he knew anything.

❖❖❖

After a light breakfast of toast and jam, where they had gone over the events of the night before it was decided Mike would stay and help her with the kitchen. The window the burglar had used wasn't damaged, it had just been left unlocked allowing him to force it open. The screen was another matter. Two of its pins holding the screen in the frame were bent and needed straightening before it could be placed back in the window. In the meantime, Kit agreed it was best to keep all first-floor windows locked at night from now on. Mike would take the screen back to his shop and see if he could repair it.

"Sanding or priming?" asked Mike. Kit looked around the kitchen. The long wall-cabinet, minus its doors, hung securely above the counter on the one side of the room she hadn't tackled yet. There were still doors to prime and one set of base cabinets next to the fridge that had been sanded and were ready for their next coat.

"Umm…priming," she said.

"Very well. Point me to the step ladder."

They worked in silent companionship, each with their own thoughts about recent events. By two o'clock, they had finished the cabinets, leaving them ready to apply the final coat of melamine white paint.

"It's going to look great when the doors are back on," said Mike, admiring their work.

"Yes, I think so too. What do you think about glass doors?"

"I think it would create a different style for your kitchen; more country, maybe."

"Hmm, yes, you're probably right. I'll wait and ask Pat for her opinion."

"What about going for a walk down to the town, and have a"—he checked the kitchen clock—"late lunch or early supper?"

"I'd like that. Give me five minutes."

They walked down the main street in the opposite direction they had walked to the pond, passed homes that were new and many more that were old, adding to the heritage aspect of the town. "This is the first time I've walked down the street to the town since I moved in," said Kit. The trees on either side of the street merged creating a leafy canopy, adding shade to the sidewalk areas.

They passed many other people, almost all walking their dogs. "I guess I'll have to get a dog," said Kit, then laughed.

"It does look as if you need a dog in order to live here."

They walked for about fifteen minutes admiring the yards of the homes along the way.

The beach ran perpendicular to the town and on a beautiful sunny day like today the water's edge was crowded with people enjoying the cool water. A younger crowd played volleyball in the sand, while many still-younger children attempted to build sand castles in the damp sand.

They walked along the sandy edge, so as not to get dry sand in their shoes, looking for coloured glass and shells. Kit reached down to a beautiful stone she had found. Coloured a goldy-brown colour, it had specks of gold glitter reflecting the light. She reached down to pick it up and it dissolved in her fingers. "Ewe, yuck. It's bird poop!"

Mike burst out laughing. "Let's *hope* that's what it was." Kit washed her hand at the water's edge and laughed along with Mike. They gave up looking for interesting finds and they walked down the beach to the pier. The pier was long and half way up was banked on either side by humungous rocks. Some fishermen had stepped carefully and were perched on rocks waiting for a bite, while one man standing close to the end of the pier was patiently reeling in a large salmon he'd caught, while others looked on in admiration.

The lake was calm today with the look of blue steel. There were only a few smaller sailing boats out on the lake hoping for enough of a breeze to enjoy the day. Two large lakers were anchored out in the middle of the lake, waiting their turn to enter the nearby canal. On the other side of the channel, a white lighthouse with red trim stood tall, guarding the entrance.

Reaching the end of the pier, they stood for a while watching a man on a Sea Doo crisscross the waves he made, enjoying the jumping effect they caused. Looking back toward the town, they watched as a fishing charter boat arrived back at its docking area, then waited to see if any of the men that had gone fishing had caught anything substantial. They walked slowly back toward the town, ready for their supper. The park adjacent to the beach started to fill up with families, intending a leisurely picnic to staying at home. Some fathers made use of the small charcoal bar-be-cues that the park offered, while children ran around chasing the many resident geese. One little girl was chased by an angry mother goose after she went too close to her goslings.

There were many restaurants open offering a quick meal, some others opening later for the supper hour with more elaborate dishes.

"This looks good," said Mike. He read the menu attached to the door of the restaurant. It was a menu specializing in seafood. "How does shrimp and chips sound?"

"Perfect."

They sat in the upper deck of the building enjoying their shrimp meal as others began entering the restaurant for their evening meal.

"I liked Liam McQuarrie," said Kit.

"Me too. He's a bit different from what I remembered. But I think we can trust him."

He gave his last piece of shrimp a final bite. "This was good, I'm full. Would you like dessert?"

Kit leaned back against her chair. "I couldn't eat another bite right now. I have some cheese cake at home, we could have some a little later." She looked over the railing at the traffic below. Cars were entering the small town, ready to enjoy the night life.

"Sounds good." Mike waved to the server implying they were finished, when Kit's phone made the melodious sound of an incoming call.

"Hello? Yes, just finishing supper. All right, tomorrow at ten, the same address. Thank you. Bye."

Mike looked at her expectantly during the conversation, and guessed the caller. "He's found something?"

Kit smiled. "Yes, and he's coming over tomorrow morning to discuss his findings."

Back at Kit's house they sat in the living room contemplating, what Liam McQuarrie could possible have found, while sharing a small cheesecake.

"He must have found something interesting, and obviously too involved to discuss it over the phone."

"Maybe he found our fisherman was actually a famous artist after all. Wouldn't that be great."

Mike chuckled softly. "I doubt that. But I suppose we'll hear about it when he comes over."

It was getting late and Mike realized that Kit was still tired from her previous interrupted night and wanted to give her a chance to relax and get to bed earlier if she wanted. "I'll see you tomorrow, just before ten."

Kit stood up to give him a hug goodbye. He kissed her and hugged her in return. "I'll double check the doors and windows before I go. Try to get a good night's sleep."

A few minutes later Kit was watching from her front door as Mike drove away. Tomorrow might be very interesting, depending upon what McQuarrie had to say.

Chapter 9

They sat together on the front porch waiting for Liam McQuarrie to arrive. When his car pulled into her driveway behind Mike's car, they went to greet him. He raised his trunk door so Mike could carry in the painting while Kit and Liam led the way.

The formal report was paused as Kit made coffee for the three of them; while McQuarrie admired the work she'd done to the kitchen already. Once settled, McQuarrie began to tell them what he had found.

He smiled, ready to reveal his find. "It's a cotton canvas, expensive for the times, but not as expensive as linen, and certainly nothing that a fisherman might be able to afford. He obviously had a patron that helped him with his supplies." He paused for drama as his audience looked at him hopefully. "And I believe that that patron was Eugene Albert Tayler." He waited dutifully for a question to follow.

"Why do you suppose it is Eugene Albert Tayler?" asked Kit.

"Because," he smiled, "your fisherman used a canvas that had been previously painted on by Tayler."

"You mean, there's another painting underneath Kit's painting?"

"Exactly. Under imaging we found a painting by Eugene Albert Tayler. His signature E. F. Tayler was found on the bottom left corner. It seems that it was a painting he didn't find suitable and gave the canvas to his friend to use for himself, and possibly several others as well."

"Is this Tayler very famous?" asked Kit.

"I've never heard of him, and I deal in prints all the time," said Mike.

McQuarrie took a sip of his coffee before answering. He was enjoying this revelation. He smiled. "Well, his last painting sold for one hundred, eighty thousand pounds in London, two years ago."

"One hundred, eighty …"

"That's a little over 300,000 dollars," said Mike. "That explains why Saulter wants the painting, but not how he knew about it."

"Oh, probably the same way you did. The previous owners must have taken the picture to him in Mississauga to see if it had any value, and like I did, he probably used imaging techniques to look closer."

"It's obvious too that he never told Mrs. Northwood about his find," added Mike.

"Is there a way of recovering the Tayler painting," asked Kit. She realized it would mean destroying the fisherman's painting.

McQuarrie gave that some thought before answering. "Maybe, I still need to speak to our conservator about it. She's been away on vacation. If the top painting is made of a chemically different media from the original, it might be possible. If it's the same, then it will be more difficult and time consuming. I'm a little curious about our Mr. Saulter, though. I believe I shall make further inquiries. I have many acquaintances in the art world." With that he finished up his coffee and made his farewells. He would let Kit know if anything could be done about the painting.

They sat together, each with their thoughts about what McQuarrie had found out. "Can you imagine," said Kit, "if they could actually uncover the other painting."

"That might mean a lot of money," added Mike.

"I wonder what the picture subject is? Maybe it will be something I won't like."

Mike laughed. "Well, if you're going to sell it, it doesn't much matter does it? I'm sure you'd find another picture of boats to replace it."

"I guess so, but it's the fisherman's painting. It might be the only one that's survived since then."

"I suppose that's probably true. I guess you could keep it and when you're in your nineties then you could have it restored."

Kit laughed at that. "That would be a great retirement plan."

"What shall we do today," asked Mike. "Kitchen or research?"

"I think I am starting to get attached to our William Martin. Let's see what else might come up."

❖ ❖ ❖

They sat opposite each other in their usual chairs. "I'll keep working on the newspaper sites," said Mike.

"I'm going to see what kinds of paintings Eugene Albert Tayler painted. Maybe they had similar interests."

It was fifteen minutes later that Mike gave a triumphant 'yes'. "Here, April 30, 1868, an inquest into the death of William Warren Martin, murdered in an Asylum," he read from the headlines. "*Adjourned Inquest*"

Kit joined him, her hands resting gently on his shoulders as she read the article

'The adjourned inquest upon the body of William Warren Martin, who was killed on April 23, 1868, by a fellow patient, was held at the Lunatic Asylum, Friday last, before J.G. Calvin, Esq, Coroner when the following evidence was adduced.

Thomas Woodward, an attendant, at the asylum said—I was in the gallery tidying up after the patients had prepared for their morning duties in the gardens. It was custom for the non-violent lunatics to work at tasks in the asylum vegetable garden. There were twelve, including the deceased William Martin, and Fred Dunlop. There was a loud shriek from one of the lunatics and suddenly others took up the alert that something had happened. When I reached the garden, the garden attendant was wrestling with Fred Dunlop as he held a shovel over Martin, prepared to strike again.

James Robertson, foreman of the jury: Is it safe practice to allow lunatics to use such tools?

Thomas Woodward: It is, but only those that have shown no tendency to physical violence. They are kept together in one block. William Martin was delusional and loud at times and believed he was sent from God to convert others. Fred Dunlop seemed to be his best friend. They worked together, shared their food and talked for hours, while reading the Bible.

Gilbert Reid Assistant Medical Officer, said: On Sunday the 24th I made a post mortem of the deceased by opening up the head, chest and body. I found the chest all healthy. The heart and lungs were apparently

healthy. The abdominal viscera healthy. Upon opening the head, I found effusion of blood on the surface of the brain at the base and also at the upper extremity of the spinal cavity. The skull was extensively fractured in several places which I have no doubt was caused by violence. The cause of death; injury to the head, fracture of the skull, effusion of blood on the brain resulting from a violent attack.

The coroner in summing up said: Although the accused Fred Dunlop was a lunatic, the injury inflicted was wilfully intended. The Coroner's Jury had no power to inquire into the question of sanity or insanity. Nor had the legislature invested them with power to dispose of the prisoner; and from the conclusive nature of the evidence, he considered that no other verdict than that of 'Wilful murder' against Fred Dunlop could be returned.

A verdict of Wilful Murder against Fred Dunlop was accordingly returned.'

"Oh, my," said Kit. "I wonder what happened to Fred Dunlop?"

Mike took her hand that had rested on his shoulder and gave it an affectionate pat. "Well, I did read on the Old Baily site that a lunatic just stayed in the asylum if crimes were committed or maybe transferred to another asylum. So, he wasn't put in a regular jail."

"I just hope he didn't murder anyone else. But I suppose we will never know."

They'd worked for another hour finding little more to add to their chart record.

"I'm surprised that they kept information like that," said Kit.

Mike shook his head slowly. "That's more than I thought we would find out about him. Sad in a way. To end like that." They were both feeling the aftermath of a death that happened long ago, yet had just been discovered. They had gotten close to the fisherman and to discover his ending had affected both of them.

As a distraction, Kit said, "I found a fire pit in the shed, this morning. Why don't you help me figure out how to use it. We can bar-be-que some hotdogs later."

"I'd like that. We need time to take in all this information."

❖ ❖ ❖

The propane firepit looked almost new and hadn't been used often by the look of the lava rocks embedded in the bowl, where flames now danced. Luckily the previous owner had left many manuals for items they had purchased and Kit found the firepit one on top of the pile. After arranging the hose and propane tank, Mike had the unit working beautifully. It felt warm as the sun went down past the neighbours garage. The first evening star shone in the south-west sky.

"Here, I'll trade you." Kit looked at her burned wiener and happily traded Mike for the one he had cooked.

"This is nice," she said. "I'm glad you figured out how the burner worked. It was nice of the couple who owned the house to leave a gas tank and all the garden tools."

Mike passed Kit her hotdog and prepared to take the well-done one off of the metal fork. "I suppose they thought you could use the things, besides if they moved into a condo or apartment, they wouldn't have a use for them anymore."

"True, and I can certainly make use of the lawnmower, even if I don't know what some of the other tools are for."

Mike laughed at that. "Give me a call, anytime, and I'll demonstrate them for you."

Kit sat back enjoying their meal. The sky was clear and you could see the Big Dipper clearly among the branches of the neighbouring trees.

Their mood, now brightened, turned back to their subject. "I suppose it was a good, if sad life," offered Kit. "I mean, he starts out with his family, then goes to a workhouse, either because his parents were dead or because they couldn't feed him. Then he's apprenticed out to a fisherman."

Mike gave her a raised eyebrow. "Well, probably a fisherman," she amended. "Hopefully a kind Master. He learns his trade, does well, takes on another young man as an apprentice and then is attacked for no real reason and is injured badly. He ends up in an asylum; delusional, but apparently harmless, has hideous treatments while he's there, and then is bludgeoned to death by his best friend."

"I suppose if you sum it up like that, yes it was a sad life. But don't remember his painting. He must have enjoyed many hours painting his favourite topic: the sea. Others obviously thought his work was beautiful, as we read in the trial." Mike sat back in his chair and looked up into the night sky; the moon just appearing from behind a neighbour's roof. I wonder how much this Eugene Albert Tayler helped him. Who knows how many paintings are out there with a double X signature that might really have a Tayler underneath them?"

"I wonder what Liam's conservator will say about it when she returns to work?" said Kit.

"I don't know. Liam seemed more interested in Frank Saulter."

Mike leaned forward and took two more wieners out of the plastic bag. "Another one?"

Chapter 10

Mike leaned closer to the glass of the storm door and read the note fastened to the inside.

'Mike, use the back door entrance. Don't let the dog out. He bit a delivery man this morning and I had to take him to the hospital; the delivery man not the dog. See you soon.'

Mike chuckled to himself, then made his way along the interlock sidewalk to the back yard where he found Kit leaning over a table, paintbrush in hand. "Hi, I read your note."

Kit laughed. "That was Pat's idea. She heard somewhere on T.V. that a note like that would deter burglars."

Mike considered it. "Well, I'm sure it would make some think twice. What are you doing?"

A large concrete-like creature was spread out on the grass in three undulated segments, so it looked as if it was coming out of the ground then diving back in again, the fourth section sat on the table staring at Mike with the large soulful eyes of a sea monster. "I bought this at a garage sale this morning from a lady down the street. It's quite faded, but still in good shape; so, I thought I'd touch it up a bit before adding it to my garden. I've rubbed a darker grey-green paint onto the scaley body and the head." She added the last touch of black to the eyes and stood back. "What do you think?"

"I think it's great! Once you space out the segments it'll look like a large sea monster travelling around your yard." The large yard in question was all grass, with a chain link fence surrounding the three sides. "It's a nice, big yard. There's a lot you could do with it. Maybe some trees too."

"I'd like to eventually get a deck built and a nice wooden fence, when I can afford it. Did you have to work this morning?"

"A little. My sister took a shadow box order from an older man who wanted his medals preserved. She hasn't done anything like that before so I helped for an hour. She's set to stay until Monday, so we still have a few days to work together."

Kit smiled to herself. She felt they didn't still need the William Martin research in order for them to see each other, but recognized too, that for now Mike felt comfortable with the premise, so she would go along with that. She liked Mike for himself and wanted to continue seeing him, even if it didn't involve the painting.

"Shall I get the machines set up while you finish here?"

"Yes, thanks." Kit looked at the two segments left to paint. "I should be done in fifteen minutes." Then, as an afterthought she warned, "Watch out for the dog."

Finished her painting and leaving the sea serpent to roam about the yard, Kit came back inside and found Mike deep in thought.

"Hi, what did you find."

"Come and see." He enlarged the screen with the record so Kit could read it. "The family on the 1871 census. Emily Martin a widow and living on own means, still at the same address." Then he smiled. "I know you were wondering, so here it is; her daughter Emily M. Northwood- wife of fisherman, Grandson Ralph Northwood age 11-errand boy and Granddaughter Lydia Northwood age 8-scholar."

"Oh, Mike. That's wonderful. So, the Northwoods were family. And they kept the picture all those years."

"It seems that way." He pressed 'save' to print out a copy later for Kit to keep.

❖ ❖ ❖

"I'm glad you thought of this." Kit took another bite of her sandwich and watched the lake water, as it washed the sandy beach in front of them, one of three small beaches in the park that ran along the Service Road giving access to Lake Ontario. After Mike's Northwood discovery, he had suggested the five-minute drive to the park.

They set up their picnic area by the furthest beach where it was more secluded, allowing enough room for the two of them to stand side-by-side and cast their lures. They'd fished for an hour with no success, before deciding to stop for the picnic Mike had purchased at a local delicatessen. He'd brought food, drinks, plastic plates and cutlery, hoping to have a quiet time away from the computers.

"I'll have to remember to stop by this place," said Kit.

"Where did you live before moving here?" Mike asked.

"I had an apartment in Grimsby. I still have to drive there for work, but I like it here. A little less crowded. And I like my new house very much, and its eighteen-hundred square feet is more than enough room."

Mike laughed. "I wish I had that much room, my apartment has maybe a third of that."

Suddenly she was distracted. "What's that black thing in the water?" They were sitting on a rise overlooking their beach and could see the dark shadow of a fish swimming close to the shore.

"Maybe a salmon," suggested Mike. "Although it's pretty dark in colour for a salmon; or a trout maybe, and look at the fins; it has the shape of a baby shark." He laughed at the thought, then took out his phone to record the fish. They watched the fish for a few minutes as it swam back and forth close to the shore, then out again. "Curious."

"Do you think he might go for our lures?"

"He might." Mike picked up their rods. "Let's try, at least if we catch it, we can see what it is before letting it go."

After fifteen minutes of no luck attempting to catch the mysterious fish, they spent the rest of their time walking around the park and trying their skill with casting whenever they came to a small creek or pond, of which the park had many, that fed into the lake.

It was late afternoon when they arrived back at Kit's house, ready to look for any more clues they might discover about the fisherman's life.

Tomorrow was the last full day Mike could spend researching and helping with the cabinets until the following weekend and they wanted to make the most of it.

They were an hour into searching with nothing new to add to their chart when Pat called. She was coming over.

"Well, what do you think?" Pat held the door handles in the light of the nearest window for Kit to see.

"I think they're perfect. Like the ones I picked out, but somehow better. I think it's the nickel finish." Kit picked up one of the handles and compared the back with the mounting holes to the holes already in the cabinets doors left from the last hardware. "It shouldn't be too difficult," said Kit. "I can still use the lower hole and just fill one."

Mike sat at the kitchen bar watching this exchange with interest, a cup of coffee in his hand. Then suddenly asked for his opinion, he smiled. He didn't really have one, so thought best to be neutral in the discussion until it was finalized. "Whatever you'd like to do. I have my drill and bits still in the car." He checked the new hinges and matched them to the original cabinet holes. "These should work fine. These kinds of hinges don't seem to have changed much over the years."

"The man in the hardware section said you'd probably need some wood filler, so I picked up a can as well." Pat looked at the cabinet doors with a critical eye. It's a good thing you didn't put on the final coat yet."

"What do you think about the colour, white or an accent colour? I was even considering glass inserts."

"I think the white will work well. It will save a lot of work and you can add colour later with counter items; bowls, canisters, bread box, plants, that sort of thing."

"So, white it is," said Kit.

"I'll go and get my drill from the car. If we put the final holes in now, you can better prep the doors before the melamine coat goes on."

It was a full-moon night and Kit was still awake. Although she had had other sleepless nights, she didn't think the phase of the moon was to blame. Light edged the blinds in her room as intermittent clouds blocked the moon's glow. Kit leaned over for the tenth time and checked her night table clock—2:15—five minutes later than the last time she had checked.

There was a girl at work who suffered from insomnia and had shared her research about the topic, with the suggestion from magazines as how to overcome it. One such suggestion was to read a book for a while and if that failed, do something constructive rather than just lying there in bed thinking.

So, constructive, it would be. Kit couldn't think of anything more constructive than looking for the fisherman's family. She smiled at the thought. Tightening her robe, Kit dimmed the dining room light and opened up her laptop, preparing to look up his sons and daughters in the Barking records.

According to Mike, most people back then didn't move too far from where they were born, so she would start with the Barking records she had found on the free site, looking for marriages. Mike had found the Northwood marriage earlier. Maybe the couple had stayed there and started a family.

Entering the Barking records from the free site and knowing roughly the ages people married, Kit started in 1819 and slowly checked each page for the names she knew.

Edward, William and Joseph had left home by 1851, leaving the two girls, Elizabeth and Emily May, so maybe between 1841 and 1851 they might have married. Then remembering what Mike had said; just because they weren't on the '51 census, doesn't mean they didn't live there. So maybe they were somewhere in the north Atlantic. Kit had visions of the boys hauling in fish of the decks of the Emma.

After fifteen minutes later, Kit read the last page for the September 1843 marriages. Edward Martin— fisherman—son of William Martin—fisherman, married Eliza Davies. She smiled, she would look for Edward and Eliza up again on future census records. If he was fisherman at that time, chances were, he stayed in Barking.

She paused in her search long enough to enter the information on to the chart that still occupied the centre area of her table. She smiled thinking how pleased Mike would be when she saw him tomorrow.

She'd learned a lot in a short time and was pleased too that she'd taken that step and accepted Mike's help. She yawned. The living room mantel clock struck its soft half-hour chime—3:30.

Reading repetitious records on a small screen had had the appropriate effect of making her tired, but Kit was not quite ready to go back to bed just yet.

The next person in the marriage records was the youngest son, Joseph, who married in 1845 to a girl named Lydia Wyatt, and again the father of the groom was William Martin—fisherman, witnesses being Edward and Eliza Martin.

By four o'clock, Kit had found all the children except William, all married and probably still living in Barking by 1861.

Her eyes were beginning to tire and shortly before the mantel clock struck 4:30 Kit was finally back in bed and asleep.

Chapter 11

"It's Liam." Mike opened the text message and read aloud to Kit. '*Have spoken to our conservator. It will take time and some money but it might be done. There's a fifty-fifty chance if you wish to try to reveal the painting underneath the one you have, but if it turned out well, it would be worth it.*'

"Well, that's some encouraging news. Looks like you may have an option after all."

Kit was surprised and delighted at the news. "Yes, that is good news." But then again, it meant ruining the fisherman's picture. She had begun to feel a connection with William Martin and wasn't sure if she wanted to take the chance of discovering another more valuable painting beneath his. It would be ruining something that had meant a lot to him and his family.

"Wait, there's, more," said Mike.

There was a second message. '*I have looked into Frank Saulter. His real name is Paul Leitch. He's from London and worked there in the gallery business for five years as a conservator. Also wanted for forgery, theft and assault in the U.K., probably why he left. Liam.*'

"I wonder how he found all this out?" asked Kit.

Mike has been wondering the same thing. "I'm sure he has connections in the art world, even Britain. The assault part is a little worrisome, though."

"Maybe the police have been alerted now and are watching him."

"They might, but I think it would be wise until this is all over if you stay at Pat's or she come here." He gave her a weak smile. "Just in case, he tries again."

Kit contemplated this. "I think I'd feel safer if you were to stay over. The police report was about someone breaking in here, and as you said if he tries again, we have some proof of a prior."

"That makes sense." Mike was more than pleased with the role of protector. "I'll go home a get a few things."

"That would be fine. I could make supper and we could work a little after."

❖ ❖ ❖

There was a ding and Kit saw that she had some email yet to be opened.

"I have another email from Jennet. She's sent two attachments." Mike put down his pen and left the note he was making until after they read the messages.

'*Hi Kit. Had some time to go to Kew today. Found a certificate you might like to add to your William Martin collection. It took a while, but I was able to find some of the asylum records. Attached are copied of the notes that I made. Hope this helps. Enjoy. Jennet.*'

Kit waited for Mike to join her on her side of the table then hesitated before opening up the first attachment, almost afraid of what she might find.

Kit opened up the first one.

"Look, it's a death certificate." The information contained the usual facts listed on an English death certificate; date of death, place of death, name, sex, age, profession, cause of death, with description and

113

signature of informant which in this case, was the County Coroner.

Mike read the particulars, *"William Warren Martin died April 23, 1868, at the county Lunatic Asylum. Age: seventy-six. Profession: Labourer. Cause of Death: Fracture of the skull and effusiveness of the brain, wilful murder by a patient Fred Dunlop."*

The second attachment was a little more disturbing. Notes Jennet had taken of the doctor's findings: *William was examined on April 25, 1868. 48 hours following death, which was 5 hours after the attack. It describes in graphic detail the injuries sustained to William's head, including sizes of various wounds and the finding of bits of broken bone, and swelling of the brain. It was also observed that his heart and other organs appeared in good condition.*

"I hope he wasn't conscious for those five hours," said Kit, sad now that they had read the report. "That would have been terrible, surviving that attack."

❖ ❖ ❖

It was midnight before Kit and Mike parted for bed, Mike deciding to stay over, just in case. They'd stayed up 'till then watching a movie and then talking and sharing their ideas about the fisherman's life.

He lay on the couch watching the light that escaped through the vertical blinds of the front window. The street light catching the blades and dancing on the wall across from him. It caught the colours of the painting occasionally and his thoughts alternated between the painting and his feelings for Kit and if they would continue their relationship.

He could hear the water running upstairs as Kit got ready for bed and wondered if she was thinking the same thoughts. He straightened the blankets and tried to erase all thoughts so he could sleep.

❖ ❖ ❖

"Be careful!" whispered Frank Saulter. The man with him, a ruffian he just recently hired to help him break in, had just stumbled over a planter set by the back steps. He jimmied the door open with a soft click and the two men entered the living space next to the kitchen. He adjusted his flashlight to a softer beam and proceeded to the living room where he knew he'd find the painting. It was late, and he hoped the woman who owned the painting now would be sound asleep.

He made his way through the dining room toward the living room, in anticipation of retrieving his property. He raised his arm up to caution his accomplice. There was someone asleep on the couch. "There," he said, standing before the fireplace looking up at the fisherman's painting. "What have they done?" he said, in disbelief.

❖ ❖ ❖

Paul Leitch stared at the painting on the wall above the fireplace. It had only been four months since he had last seen the painting in London.

Mrs. Northwood, a widow, had come to his gallery, shortly after arriving from Canada.

"You see," began the elderly woman. "It was left to me by my husband's great Uncle Henry, along with other keepsakes. It has something to do with his family I believe. As I'll be going back to Canada in two week's time with the few things I have inherited, I thought I would come by and see if the painting was worth anything."

"Quite right," said Leitch. "I have an idea," he said. "Why not leave it here with me to investigate further, then I can also have it wrapped properly for transport so as not to get it damaged." He smiled. "With my compliments," he added. "I can tell you then if I have found anything about the artist and hopefully its value."

"Why, that's very kind of you," replied Mrs. Northwood. "Even if it doesn't have any monetary value, I think I shall keep it, for my husband's sake you understand."

"So, let's say in three days."

"That will be perfect. I'll see you on Thursday."

Mrs. Northwood had left the painting in its plain black frame with Paul Leitch, who upon arriving home, took the frame itself to his workshop and began, using a small rotary saw, carving out a channel along the back of three sides of the frame—a channel large enough to house the cache of rubies he had stolen a month ago. Once the rubies were embedded, it didn't take much to cover them and the remaining opening with wood filler. Then after a day of drying, he touched up the area with black paint, rubbed a mixture of sand and gravel over the newly painted area to disguise his work and the painting was ready to travel with Mrs. Northwood back to Canada.

He needed to leave England, and knew of an art dealer he'd met a few years ago that with encouragement, might give him a job, once he had arrived in Toronto. Legally he could stay six months without a visa and that was more than enough time to find the painting again. He needed a workplace for reference, once he changed his name. It wouldn't take much for him to retrieve the frame. All he'd have to do is say he had someone willing to give her a few hundred dollars for it. And if he was any judge of people; she would gladly take the money.

"It's definitely an original from around 1850," he had told her Thursday afternoon. "As there doesn't seem to be a signature I wouldn't think that the picture was painted by anyone significant. Perhaps it would fetch twenty pounds from someone who loved the subject of the work."

She seemed disappointed but not surprised by his appraisal. "That is too bad, but I'm sure it will fit in nicely with my new home. "I'm moving in a month's time when I get back. My husband's lawyer has found me a nice one-level senior's bungalow. He thinks my home in St. Catharines is much too big for me to take care of on my own. I have a heart condition you see, and it's been difficult since my husband passed away."

"I'm sorry to hear that," he said, trying to sound sincere. "I have an art dealer friend in Mississauga. I will tell him about your painting. Perhaps he can find a client who might be interested in buying it."

"Oh, that would be wonderful," she said. "I can't thank you enough for your kindness, Mr. Leitch."

"Not at all. I hope you have a pleasant trip."

With that Mrs. Northwood had taken with her a fortune in rubies. A fortune he was determined to recover.

Now he stood in front of the painting, in disbelief. It had been newly reframed.

◆ ◆ ◆

"What have they done?" A voice heard in the dreamy, half-awake state of an interrupted sleep. Mike rolled over, suddenly aware that there was someone in the room with him. He blinked his eyes and saw a man standing in front of him. Startled, he attempted to get up and confront the intruder, and was pushed back down by the strong arm of a burly man.

"Kit, call the police!" he called. He hoped that would stall the thieves progress and may even scare them off. He attempted to get up again, intending to fight off the man who had accosted him. There was a second man and Mike recognized the face he'd seen before on the internet and at Kit's home. Frank Saulter, standing in front of the fireplace, called to the large man who had confronted him.

"Kit …" Mike tried to call a warning and was rewarded with a punch to his jaw and then a second to the mid-section, which caused him to double up and crumple onto the couch.

Upstairs, Kit woke to the sounds from the living room below. She heard Mike's second chance to warn her and could see the flashlight beams reflecting up the staircase onto her office walls. Hearing the men below and fearful that Mike had been hurt, she called out, "The police are on their way!" hoping it would induce the thieves to leave, with or without the painting, for they certainly must have returned intending to steal it.

"Mike! Are you all right?" Kit heard a door slam shut, then ventured a look down the staircase. It was dark, the flashlight that had searched the room, gone now. Her ruse seemed to have worked. She heard a moan from below.

She ran down the stairs that led to the hallway and then the dining room, so she could turn on the lights on her way down to the living room and Mike.

She found Mike sprawled on the couch, trying to recover from the punches he'd taken. "Oh, Mike." Kit went to his side as he staggered, trying to stand up.

"I'm okay," he said, "just had the air knocked out of me."

"Here, sit back down." She assessed the damage to his face and saw the red swelling on the side of his jaw. "I'll call the police now."

"What do you mean, now?" he asked.

Kit smiled. "I just yelled that out hoping they'd run away. And it seemed to work."
Then a thought occurred to her. "Were you able to get a look at them?"

"Yes. It was Saulter, or should I say Leitch, and another guy. I don't think I'd care to meet his associate again." He rubbed his face cautiously, checking for loose teeth.

Kit was on the phone, having dialed 911. She gave the police a brief description as to what had happened and after assuring the desk officer that no one had been seriously hurt and the thieves had fled, waited as the dispatcher arranged for an officer to come over and make a report.

Once off the phone, Kit turned the ceiling light on, then joined Mike on the couch. "Here, let me see." She turned his face, better to see the cut lip and bruised jaw. He tried to smile, his face wincing at the effort. "What happened?"

Mike shook his head slightly. "I'm not too sure. I was sleeping and then I heard a voice which woke me. It was Saulter, he said something strange. I tried to get up to confront him and a big guy pushed me down. That's when I called to you. Then he flattened me when I tried to get up again."

"You're sure it was Saulter."

"Very. I never saw the big guy before, though."

"You lie back and rest. I'll get you some ice, then watch for the police."

It didn't take long for a police vehicle to pull into her driveway. A familiar face appeared at the door; Officer Anders.

Kit opened the screen door. "Come in, won't you."

"You stated in your call that the thieves had fled," he said, having a quick look around the living room. He acknowledged Mike sitting on the couch, with a makeshift ice pack on his face.

"Yes. They did assault Mr. Reynolds in the process of stealing my painting, but left when I shouted down that the police were coming."

He smiled at that. "Very ingenious. You're lucky it worked." He took out his note book and pen. "So, start at the beginning."

Mike began the story, brief as it was and Kit continued, up until the part where she had called the police.

"You're sure you recognized one of the men?"

"Yes," said Mike. "Frank Saulter. He's been trying to buy the painting from Kit." Then as an after thought he added, "You can see his picture on the internet, he works for Scottlea Art Gallery in Mississauga."

Officer Anders took notes then looked at the painting in question. "You must have woken in time to stop them from taking it."

"I suppose so."

Then more formally Anders asked, "Do you wish to press charges against this Mr. Saulter? For assault," then looking at Kit he added, "or for the breaking and entering?"

That hadn't occurred to either he or Kit, and now faced with the question, Mike hesitated. "I'd like to think about it first," said Mike. "Can I come down to the station tomorrow to fill out the necessary forms?"

Officer Anders looked at the swelling on Mike's face and nodded. "Of course. I'll make note of it here."

"If you have any questions, you can call the station. Before I go though, I'd like to see the damage to the back door, and take a few pictures."

Kit nodded in agreement. "I'll show you to the back." After recording everything necessary, Kit walked Officer Anders along the side pathway, back to his car. She was glad he was the police office who had shown up, then for a moment thought there might be an ulterior motive.

Mike leaned back on the couch, his lip and jaw numb from the ice. He was tired and sore, but his mind kept going back to the phrase he had heard, or thought he'd heard, until sleep had overwhelmed him.

Chapter 12

Mike woke to the smell of bacon cooking in the kitchen. Kit had let him rest and it was close to ten before he had roused from sleep. His jaw ached and his lip was tender but he was hungry nonetheless; maybe a few pieces of bacon if he chewed carefully, and maybe an egg, toast would be nice too, he thought. So, he prepared for the day ahead, their last full day before he went back to work tomorrow.

"Do we go to the police station today?" asked Kit, as she set the breakfast plate in front of Mike.

"I don't want to, but I think we probably should." He sampled the breakfast plate and sighed in satisfaction, a half piece of bacon in his hand.

Mike looked no better this morning. His lip was puffed and his skin was a dark bluish colour where he'd been hit.

"I suppose we should tell them everything we know about Frank Saulter," suggested Kit.

"Probably. Let's finish breakfast, then go. I'd just as soon get it over with."

By one o'clock they were back at Kit's house, having explained everything they knew about Frank Saulter, and his alias; Paul Leitch and the painting.

Mike was unable to charge Frank Saulter with assault because he wasn't the one who hit him. As to a charge of break and enter, thanks to Officer Ander's photos, they were able to show that a break-in took place, and although an indictable offence was not committed, the intent to commit an offence, that is:

stealing the painting, was corroborated by the previous break-in report. With the incident noted and on record, Kit decided not to formally charge anyone with breaking and entering.

Once back at Kit's, they sat in the kitchen, reviewing the events of the previous night.

Mike was feeling better, but puzzled over what had happened. "I wish I could remember what it was Saulter was saying when I woke up."

"Do you have an idea in what context he was speaking? Maybe he was talking to the other guy."

Mike shook his head slowly, thinking. "No, he sounded as if he was upset about something."

"Something, the other guy did?"

"I don't think so, he was staring at the picture when I looked up. They had time to take the picture, but they didn't. Even after you called down, they could have snatched it and run. Why didn't they?"

"Maybe they tried before you woke up. Remember we did attach it to the wall with wire and an extra screw."

He smiled at that. "True, that's probably it." Then to change the subject, he said, "What do you feel like doing today."

"Well, I can check first to see if Jennet has sent any more emails. We could gather all our William Martin information and organize it into some sort of history, while adding in all the actual historical things we've found. It might be interesting to look into the Northwood family as well, now that we know there is a family connection to the painting."

Mike leaned back in his chair considering Kit's suggestions. "This is our last full day together; so, yes, let's finalize everything we've found. I doubt we find anything more about his paintings, though."

Kit turned on her computer while Mike rewrote their findings from the sheet of paper stretched out across the table. He began a double-spaced history of William Martin, adding in titles of historical content between lines, corresponding to the dates they had.

Then a thought occurred to him. He opened up his computer and typed in the search section; double X signature on oil paintings. A moment later there was a single link suggesting someone had an unknown-artist's painting for sale on eBay.

"Kit, look!"

Mike opened the page and saw at the top, a picture of boats; smacks in a harbour, not unlike the painting Kit had now in her living room.

A guy named Howard, in Alberta had it for sale for sixty-five dollars. The description said it had been purchased while on a trip to Britain and admitted it was by an unknown artist.

"That's amazing," said Kit. "I'd like to message him and let him know who the artist actually is. Maybe there are more of Martin William's works out there. Oh, and I wonder if that means there are more undiscovered works by Eugene Albert Tayler? Wouldn't that be something."

Mike laughed at the idea. "That *would* be something. Imagine how surprised this Howard would be to learn that he might have a rare valuable picture. Yes, let's message him."

Twenty minutes later after informing Howard about the true identity of his painting and how he could get it checked at a local gallery, Kit had received a brief response to her message: '*OMG, I just sold it!*'

Mike laughed. "Oh no, I wonder if he will pass the message on or try to get out of the sale?"

Kit was still laughing. "I guess we'll never know." She checked her inbox. "An email from Jennet."

Mike came around to her side of the table. He put his hands on her shoulders and gave a warm squeeze of affection.

"It's from the hospital's case notes. Jennet will send the full documents later after she goes back to the library. These are the notes she made from what she read."

It was an asylum record regarding some of his behaviour and even sadder some of the treatments they had tried. Kit read the notes that Jennet had taken.

The Case Notes cover several years-1859 to 1868

William was stated as married and a fisherman from Barking.

April 12, 1859, about 3 weeks before his admission,

William Warren Martin was committed for one month to the House of Correction in Ilford in the county of Essex, for vagrancy.

He often rambled as if talking to himself, sometimes in a very agitated state. He was incoherent at times and delusional. He said God told him what to do. He was to read the Bible to as many people as he could, whenever he had the chance and, if he did this,he would get to Heaven.

He worked in the laundry until he escaped in August of 1862, and walked as far as Dagenham. He was allowed to work on the farm after that, where they could keep an eye on him and where his noisy ramblings wouldn't annoy anyone else.

He often wrote to his family telling them how badly he was being treated, stating he was being starved and beaten. He never had visitors. He would have loud violent outbursts occasionally. Blisters applied to the nape of the neck had quieted him somewhat. Other times, a restraining device had been used to prevent him from possibly harming others or himself when confronted. When not working, he reads his Bible.

There was also information about the murderer and his relationship with William Martin.
Fred Dunlop was admitted September 5th 1860, that's about a year after William was admitted. Once he was assigned to the same quarters as William Martin, the two were seldom seen apart. Dunlop suffered from debilitating migraines and believed Martin could cure him with the words of the Bible.

He was removed from the asylum after the murder, then returned three weeks later. He was finally removed to a different asylum two months after that. At the asylum, when he was asked why he had attacked William Martin, he said, 'God had told him to do it.'

Both were silent after reading the last paragraph, then Mike concluded, "I guess there's no more to it, really, is there. A sad ending to a decent man."

127

"Yes, I wonder what became of his family after he died. It's sad they seemed to abandon him. Maybe the wife remarried."

"Maybe, although the kids were grown by then and she still had her nursing to get by on. But don't forget too, there was a social stigma to having a husband and father in a lunatic asylum. It might be interesting to follow the family later."

Kit smiled; she would like that. She enjoyed spending time with Mike. "You know, I just realized I haven't called Pat yet about all this excitement. We've been so busy since last night." It was close to two o'clock. She reached for her cellphone. "She should be at the house now."

"I think I need a glass of wine," said Mike. "My jaw is still a bit sore."

"It's been a rough day. Thanks, I can use this." Pat took a sip of her wine. "The painters screwed up and painted two rooms the opposite colour. Then I said to the head painter, 'What have you done? This is going to set us back a day at least.' He just shook his head and said he'd get it done."

"I'm sure it will all work out okay," said Kit. She looked at Mike who seemed to be staring into nothing, hypnotized. "What is it, Mike. Mike?"

The trance broken, he looked at Kit, sudden realization on his face. "That's it! That's what I heard that woke me. 'What have they done?' That's what Saulter said. He was upset and looking at the picture, and said, 'What have they done?'"

"What do you suppose he meant," asked Pat.

"Maybe he was referring to Mrs. Northwood?"

"Maybe," considered Mike, "but the only thing that seems to have been changed, is the frame, and we did that."

Kit looked at Pat. "Where is the frame, Pat?" She had loaned it to her, shortly after Pat had her new assignment.

Pat looked at both of them, a little nervous at giving her answer. "I wanted to show the wood guy I'm working with what an 1850s frame looked like. He was considering embellishments on the wainscoting and wanted something more historic …"

"Where is the frame now?" said Kit and Mike in unison, interrupting her reasoning.

Suddenly, Pat looked flustered. "I'll find it."

"Do it! Now!" said Kit.

Pat grabbed her purse and keys from the counter. "I'll be right back."

"What could it be?" asked Kit. "What is so important about that frame?"

"We won't know until we see it. But Saulter obviously thinks it's important, so let's hope she finds it."

It took an hour before a nervous Pat returned with the frame in tact. They sat at the kitchen bar with the frame flat on the counter, each wondering what it was Saulter could possibly want with this old frame.

"Maybe there's something hidden in the frame," offered Kit.

Mike looked at the frame critically. "It doesn't seem to have been tampered with, but that doesn't mean a clever person who knows a lot about forgery and conservation couldn't do it. He ran his hand along the edges, feeling for any irregularity other than the dents and scratches of time. Finding nothing suspicious, he did the same along the flat edges and sides of the frame. Again, he could feel no difference that suggested that the frame had been altered.

The girls watched as he conducted his examination. "Maybe Liam could use his x-ray machine to check along the sides?" suggested Kit.

Mike shook his head. "I don't know. Years ago, I had a sliver of wood wedged in my hand and I went for an x-ray but it couldn't detect wood. Maybe he could detect something that wasn't wood, though."

"Why don't we just take it apart?" offered Pat.

Kit looked at Mike and they both looked at Pat and laughed.

"I saw a hand saw in the basement," said Kit.

"It's your call," said Mike, giving Kit a raised eyebrow in question.

Kit contemplated that. "Well, normally I would say save it, because it's the original frame, but considering the circumstances I think we have no option but to take it apart."

"Great!" said Pat, eager to see if something was actually there.

The frame lay on a work bench surrounded by three uncertain faces, like doctors hesitating to perform surgery upon a waiting patient with an unknown ailment. "Where do we start?" asked Kit.

Mike picked up the saw, then set it down and replaced it with a hammer. "We should probably separate it at the corners first. I'll use the hammer; I'd rather not cut through anything that might be important. With a nod of agreement from Kit, Mike tapped the inner corners of the frame. It was old and the joints were loose, so the four sides came apart easily. "There, now we can examine each side piece separately."

The girls each picked up a section of frame and visually looked for anything unusual. Other than the dents and discolouration of the paint with age, there didn't seem to be anything unusual in the wood. "How should we take them apart now?" asked Pat.

"Wood has a grain," said Mike. He felt along the painted surface. "I suggest we scrape off the paint layer and see if the wood underneath has been altered in any way."

Mike looked around the small workshop, where the previous owners had left many of their tools; not needing them in their new home. He opened up a drawer and found smaller tools and among them, a wide chisel; which he thought would work.

Mike picked up the chisel, and carefully scraped off the old paint from the flat surfaces of the frame piece. Sandpaper hung from a board on the wall and he took down a piece of medium grit, and handed it to Kit. "Try this in the grooved parts, while I try the next piece."

He picked up another frame section and started to scrape off the paint. The paint here came off easily where it had been primed recently. "Look!" He pushed the blade a little deeper and revealed the wood filler that had sealed up a wide lengthwise trench in the wood. "I don't think they had wood filler in 1840. Someone has recently made a repair of some sort here."

"Try the other two sides first," suggested Kit.

"This is exciting," added Pat, moving her long hair out of the way, as she leaned forward to look closer.

Mike repeated the procedure on the remaining two sides and on both found that they had been altered in the same way and repaired with wood filler. Using the point of the chisel, Mike scored the wood filler repeatedly until he had made a small indentation. The wood filler concealed an area about eight inches by almost an inch. Slowly he chipped away the hardened filler.

Everyone watched in anticipation as the filler finally crumbled away revealing a small trench that was filled with a film of white plastic.

"I suppose they didn't have plastic back in 1840 either," said Pat.

"There's a slotted screw driver on the bench, Kit."

Kit smiled. "Are you sure you wouldn't rather have a Phillips or maybe a Robertson screwdriver?" Kit laughed, then handed the slotted screwdriver to Mike.

Mike gave her a look, that said, 'very funny', then took the screwdriver. "I think we found something," he said and carefully lifted out the small irregular-shaped bundle. Once on the table he opened up the plastic and in doing so, released the contents. Rubies. Beautiful, dark, blood-red, matching rubies. Their facets sparkled in the light of the workshop.

It was quiet for a moment after the initial intake of breath from all three, as they saw the treasure. "No wonder he wanted that picture,' said Kit.

After checking the other sides of the frame, four small packets of rubies sat on the work shop table.

"Are rubies worth much?" asked Pat. "I thought diamonds were more valuable."

"Some rubies are rare and far more valuable than diamonds," said Kit. When given a look by Pat, she added, "I saw a documentary on Burma once. Their dark rubies are very rare."

Mike nodded slowly, realizing the danger they had been in. He glanced at the shop door as if expecting Saulter and his minion to suddenly materialize. "Now Saulter has two options, that is if he hasn't been picked up by the police yet. He will think you still have the frame or worse for him, that you threw it away. Either way, he will have to come back to find out for sure."

"We should tell the authorities about what we've found," said Kit.

"Yes, I suppose we should call the police. Maybe the RCMP, they deal with international crime, or the Ontario Provincial Police, they investigate Ontario crime," suggested Mike.

"Or, maybe we should consult Liam first and ask how he knew of the crimes Saulter, I mean Leitch, is wanted for in England. He must have found the information somewhere." She fingered some of the rubies in the table. "These must be stolen gems. There must be some news of them in England."

Mike considered this as sound. "I suppose, I could call Liam and ask him. Then we should probably contact the RCMP."

A plan agreed upon, Kit placed the rubies in a metal can she found in the workshop that had held a variety of washers. After dumping the washers, she cleaned out the tin with a paper towel and gently laid the stones on a fresh piece of folded paper towel, then placed the tin can on a shelf in the workshop.

Chapter 13

"Thank you, Liam." Mike returned to the kitchen where the girls waited. Mike took a seat at the counter, where Kit handed him a glass of white wine.

"Well?" asked Kit.

"He said, he had seen a picture of Saulter when he was searching for fellow curators. After our discussion, he remembered the name then searched further, having reconfirmed the name based upon what I had told him about the Mississauga gallery. Then he contacted galleries in London and found Saulter's former London employer, and found out a lot more."

"I told him about the rubies and he suggested that we contact the RCMP, and to feel free to use his discoveries as a reference, if they needed further information."

"Well, I guess that decides it," said Kit. I'll check on the internet for a number to call."

"I need to get back to the house," said Pat. "Keep me updated."

It was two hours after Kit had called the number she had found, that an officer from the Royal Canadian Mounted Police showed up at Kit's door. Sergeant McLeod was not the typical Mountie you thought of when picturing the famous Musical Ride with Mounties on horseback. She was young, and just a little past Kit's five foot eight inches. Her dark hair was tidily placed under her hat, and gone was the famous scarlet serge coat with iconic riding breeches and felt hat that—like many people—Kit had supposed they wore all the time.

Other than her insignia, and gold band on her hat with matching gold stripe along the outside seam of her dark, navy-blue pants, she looked very similar to the other police officers Kit had seen.

Sergeant McLeod took down all the information they had. After a lengthy statement incorporating both break-ins, their trip to the local police department, Liam's information about Saulter/Leitch, and finally the box of rubies found in the frame; Sergeant McLeod assured Kit and Mike that they would follow up with their counterparts in London. In the meantime, a local police officer would be assigned to watch the premises, until they located Paul Leitch alias Frank Saulter. She took photos of the rubies and frame pieces and itemized the contents of the tin box then gave Kit a receipt for their acquisition.

◆ ◆ ◆

"I'm glad it decided not to rain, I think we needed a distraction, after everything that's happened," said Mike. They walked their usual route toward the pond, fishing poles in hand, with a small box of lures carried in Kit's bag. They had had a hasty meal of burgers and french fries, then decided a leisurely walk was in need.

"You need to be back in your shop tomorrow." They passed a large stone home with a wooden picket fence almost covered with a wisteria vine, it's flowers about to bloom.

"Yes, and I think you need to stay somewhere else tonight, in case Saulter comes back."

"I'll be all right. The police will be watching the house," reasoned Kit. She stopped to pick up a blue jay's feather; a small blue and white feather that had fallen at the edge of the sidewalk. Mike stopped and waited as Kit studied the feather, then let it drop slowly on to the grass.

He stood their rods against a tree, then took her by the shoulders and turned her to face him. "Look, I don't want anything to happen to you. Saulter is desperate, and police or no police, I want you out of the house until he is captured."

Kit gave him a surprised look at that final remark. "*You* want …"

He covered her mouth with his in a passionate kiss, not caring if drivers of passing cars noticed or not. "Yes," he said. "So, whether that means you stay with Pat, or stay at my place, or go to a hotel for a few days, it's best you're not there, when he comes back. And he will."

Her face softened at this and she smiled, touched by his declaration. She looked into his hazel eyes, intent with concern. "All right." She took his free arm as they continued their walk. "Your place then, but just a couple of nights. I don't intend to let Saulter drive me away from my home for long."

"Good. Now, we have a good hour, let's do some serious fishing. Later we can pick up some groceries and you can pack whatever you might need. Then call Pat and let her know."

❖❖❖

"You know you're welcome here anytime," said Pat, "but I'm glad you'll be with Mike. Okay, give me an address and phone number." Kit had given Pat all the necessary information before driving with Mike to his place.

She didn't know what to expect after arriving at Mike's shop and going through to the back stairs that led to his apartment, but it wasn't this. Most men who lived alone had fairly sparce furnishings, often with exercise and sports equipment cluttering up the floor area or so she had thought, but here the walls were covered with framed works of art, mostly nature pictures. The few tables in the living room section, were stacked with historical books and articles, and tastefully matched carpets enhanced the space. Kit walked slowly around the living room as Mike watched. The layout was open concept with the kitchen at one end overlooking the yard in the side. A short hall led to the bedroom and small bathroom.

Kit approached the hall when a young woman emerged from the bedroom tidying her hair with a clip. "I wondered when you'd finally get back," she said in a mock scolding. "You have several orders waiting for your expertise." Then she laughed, and addressed Kit. "You must be Kit. I'm Rachel, Mike's sister."

She didn't look a lot like Mike; her hair colouring a light auburn, his a dark brown. Their eye colour was different too, but they had the same smile. "Nice to finally meet you, Rachel. Mike says you've been holding down the fort for him, while we've had our adventure."

Rachel gave Mike a sly look and he laughed. "All right, we'll tell you everything that's happened," said Mike.

After her briefing, Rachel looked concerned. "So, you think he'll come back again tonight, to find out for sure what happened to the frame."

"Mike thinks so, hence his house guest." She smiled at the look on Rachel's face. "Personally, I think I'd be fine at home. There is a police presence supposedly watching my house, just in case."

"Well, I'm glad you're here, anyway." She glanced toward the bedroom as her son made a fussing sound. "I better be going; it's late, Jimmy will be waiting for us when he gets home from work. I remade your bed and did the laundry for you."

"Thanks, Sis. Thanks for everything."

Rachel, picked up her bags ready to leave. "I hope everything works out all right Kit. It was nice meeting you." She gave her brother a knowing look. "And if you need any clarification about the orders, give me a call. Oh, and there's food in the fridge."

She went into the bedroom and picked up her small son, still in the process of waking from a nap.

Mike walked her to the door. "Night, Sis; and thank you for looking after the shop."

Rachel smiled at her brother, and with a free hand brushed his cheek. "I like her. I'll call you tomorrow."

Mike turned back to Kit after saying good night to his sister. "Some wine?"

"Thank you, yes. It's been a long day. I'm glad we went fishing. That's the first carp I ever caught, little as it was." She took the glass Mike offered her. "It didn't look too much like Goldie though."

They'd reached the pond, hoping to have the area to themselves, and were rewarded with the soft sounds of birds chirping and frogs splashing and, absent were the dedicated grandfather and boy they had met before. They sat for a while just enjoying the early evening, listening to the creatures of the pond.

"Do your parents live in town?" Mike asked as he prepared their rods.

"No, they originally went to Vancouver with my brother to help him set up a new business. They liked the area so much they decided to move there." She smiled ruefully. "At least now I have a place to visit out west, if I want."

She looked curiously at the bait he was attaching to the hooks. "When did you have time to get those?" she asked. Her nose wrinkled at the smell of garlic that wafted from the sandwich bag that contained the coloured mini marshmallows.

"I got them the day we learned about them." He finished fastening the small treats and handed a rod to her. "Are you ready to try?"

Kit gave him a dubious look. "I suppose it will save the lives of some worms." She laughed at the thought of a cartoon fish looking at her bait, wondering what it could be. It looked silly but Kit was willing to give it a go, and was surprisingly rewarded with a tug on her first cast. Together they had many tugs that resulted in marshmallows disappearing, but only one small carp had been foolish enough to get caught and was promptly released to rejoin his friends.

They sat on their bench, watching a family of mallard ducks playing in the water at the far end of the small island in the pond.

"I've had a great time this week, working with you," said Mike. He glanced at her and then away, wondering if she would respond with a similar declaration.

Kit squeezed his hand next to her and smiled. "Me too. I can't believe how much has happened since I brought my painting to you."

Mike took her hand in both of his, looking into her blue eyes. "I'd like this to continue, no matter what happens. I'd like to get to know you better." He drew her to him and kissed her gently. Kit nodded, and he kissed her again, to the applause from the bridge of the grandfather and his young grandson.

Now they were in Mike's apartment, hoping to hear something that would tell Kit it was safe to go home again. Told that a Regional Police Officer would be keeping an eye on her house, Kit had called and left information about her temporary location, along with her cellphone number, in case anything came of the surveillance.

Mike lay on the couch, his makeshift bed, thinking. He had tried to find out how much the blood-red rubies might be worth. After checking several sites, he had determined that with the number, size and colour of the gem stones they'd found, Saulter had hidden close to a quarter of a million dollars worth in the frame. Mike realized too that Saulter knew he'd been seen at Kit's house, but luckily didn't know he'd been recognized by Mike.

Mike heard a noise from the bedroom and noticed the light was still on. She hadn't gone to sleep yet either. Mike couldn't blame her; a lot had happened and she was probably worried about her home, but he was glad she was here. Kit still had a week of her vacation left and if Saulter wasn't caught he hoped she'd spend some of it with him.

Chapter 14

He glanced at the clock on his side table; almost two. Another sound caught his attention. It seemed to be coming from downstairs and then dismissed it as being his neighbours deciding to come back early from their weekend excursion. He lay back on his pillow unable to stop thinking about Saulter.

What would Saulter do if he did return to Kit's house and had searched and didn't find the old frame. He was glad now that Sergeant McLeod had taken the frame pieces as well, that way Saulter wouldn't know they'd found the rubies. But what would he do then? Would he just give up? No, he would try to …

Mike grabbed his robe and went to the bedroom. The door to the bedroom swung open with a thud against the wall. "Kit! Kit!" he called.

"What is it?" Kit asked, as she turned on the nightstand light.

"Kit, he's going to come here … Saulter," he said, hurrying to turn off the bedroom light.

"What?" Kit was tired and lack of sleep had made her think she had misheard. "Why, he doesn't know I'm here." They had made several detours on their way to Mike's place watching for any suspicious cars on the way, and felt secure that they hadn't been followed.

"No, but he knows, *I'm* here."

Kit shook her head slowly, not understanding. "How could he know that. Oh, because of the estate guy; Jenkins? You didn't give him your name, so how could he know?"

Mike was getting restless, and started to walk around the room. "It's the painting. If Saulter removes it from the wall, he'll come here next."

"Why, I don't see…"

Mike took a deep breath and explained. "On the back is my business label, it has my name and address. If he finds nothing at your house, he'll think the old frame is here, maybe in the garbage or still in my shop, he won't know until he looks."

Kit looked worried now. "And if he brings his muscle with him, he may get violent if he finds you." Then offered hopefully, "But he won't know you live here too."

"True, for the moment, but he'll know my name and try to find me."

There was another loud sound from below his apartment, as if something had been toppled. It might have been his neighbours, but they wouldn't be lingering around their staircase; they'd be in their apartment by now. No, it was someone else, in the shop.

Mike put his finger to his lips, cautioning silence. Kit came closer to him and put her arm around his waist. "Mike, I'm frightened," she whispered.

He took her arm in his, hoping to calm her. "Don't worry." There was another sound downstairs, a sound of something wooden being overturned. Then a similar sound from outside. He moved to the kitchen window that overlooked the side of his property, where a large garbage receptacle sat ready to be picked up when full. He moved the drapes just enough to peek out. It was dark and moonless with the clouds covering the sky, but he was able to see a dark shape near the bin.

"Get your phone," he whispered.

There was a sound of breaking glass from his shop and more aggressive sounds of things being tossed about.

Kit went to the bedroom, and removing her phone from its charging cord, brought her phone back to Mike.

Whispering, he said, "Go back in the bedroom and call the police. Tell them we think Saulter has followed you here, and is tearing the place apart looking for the rubies."

Kit nodded and left him at the window, while he watched for further movement from below.

Rejoining Mike, Kit touched his arm reassuringly. "They said, they would come right away."

"Good. Look." Another figure joined the one rummaging through the bin, but they could still hear noise from downstairs. "There's three of them, maybe more." There was another sound of something large being dropped, beneath them.

"If they try to come up here, they'll have to use the staircase."

Kit looked around for another exit, although she knew there wasn't one. "How can we get out?"

"The bedroom window. Both apartments have an emergency staircase that leads from the bedroom windows down to the ground. If we're quick, they won't hear us."

There was just enough light to make out shadows in the room, as the two made their way through the bedroom to the window. Mike removed the screen and wound the casement window open. With men below on the adjacent side of the building by the bin they would have to be very quiet and hope that rummaging through trash would cover any metal squeaks the staircase might make as they went down.

"Stay here," said Mike. "I'll go and listen for any sound on the stairs coming up. If it sounds as if they are intending to come up here, I'll join you and we'll leave together."

Kit nodded her understanding and waited patiently after Mike left her to go back to the living room. She was frightened, but glad now she had left her house. She could only imagine what might have happened if they had found her alone at home, and she didn't care for the outcome that scenario conjured up.

Mike stood by his living room door, waiting, listening for any sounds on the staircase that led to the two apartments. His heart skipped a beat when he heard the first sound of a heavy boot on the stairs. He stood still, frozen, listening for any sound of what the intruder, intruders—there were more than one—might do. He could hear them whispering as they approached the door, then heard a hard thud as the door to the Dutch couple's apartment gave way. He could hear the sound of items being moved as one of the men cursed having hit his leg on the sharp corner of a table. It wouldn't be long before they forced his apartment door open.

Kit was startled as Mike suddenly joined her at the window. "They're across the hall."

They could hear the sounds now of heavy footsteps. Voices, and a scuffling of feet.

There was a shout, "Stop!" Then the second word that filled Kit with relief. "Police!"

There was a scuffle at the bin outside and more figures showed up, and car headlights lit up the building from all angles, as more than one police car pulled up.

There was a knock at the apartment door. "Police! You can open the door."

Mike went to the door and was very relieved to see Officer Anders smiling at him. Kit quickly joined them. "We are very glad to see you, Officer Anders."

"They've been taken into custody. Everything should be all right now. I followed Saulter from your house, but I'm glad you called dispatch to say you were here. It allowed me to follow Saulter."

Kit looked surprised. "You mean you were the one watching my house?"

"Yes, I watched as he went in. He was there for quite a while and when he came out without the painting, well, it looked suspicious. So, rather than arrest him there, I called it in and decided to follow him. My partner stayed behind to secure your house."

He smiled at Kit. "It's all over. You should be fine now; he and his helpers are in police custody. We'll hand him over to the RCMP from here."

"We're very grateful, thank you."

❖ ❖ ❖

"I don't know about you, but I'm hungry after all this excitement."

147

Kit looked at Mike in disbelief. "You're kidding, it's three-thirty in the morning."

Mike was rummaging through the fridge freezer. "Nope. Rachel said she stocked the fridge for me." He fished out a large frozen pizza and smiled at the find. "This looks perfect. Here, you read the directions while I hunt for a baking sheet."

They sat quietly on the couch, each with their thoughts as they shared a pepperoni pizza and a bottle of beer.

Kit broke the silence, "Do you think we'll have to testify or something?"

"I don't know. I suppose we'll have to make a statement of some sort at the least. I guess it depends if there's a trial." He shook his head. "I really don't know what the protocol is for all this. Saulter did bust up my shop pretty good, so I suppose I'll have to follow up on that, as well as talk to my insurance agent."

"I'm dreading going back to my house, maybe he tore the place apart too."

"I think it will be all right. After all, there aren't too many places for you to hide a frame, and then too, why would you, you didn't know what was inside? He probably just went into each room and looked, then left."

"I hope you're right." She smiled as she took another bite, then swallowed. "You were right. I was hungry. This is so good."

Then she considered the events of the day. "You have to work tomorrow. Could you use some help?"

He drank the last of his beer, and looked at her with sincere pleasure. "Yes, I'd appreciate the help. Rachel was a better saleslady than I anticipated. I have several orders." He checked the time on the clock. "Let's get to bed and try to get a few hours sleep before I have to open tomorrow."

Kit moved closer and reached up, taking his face in her hands, and gave him a passionate kiss. "Thank you. For being there for me." She felt him tense as his arms surrounded her.

He kissed her back. They stood entwined for a moment, not moving. He wanted her to stay with him but knew too, it was too soon. Instead, he smiled at her and said, "You're welcome. Sleep well."

Mike's alarm went off at seven. Reluctantly he got up and started to prepare a light breakfast for the two of them.

"Morning," said Kit, tidying her hair, ready for a day in the framing shop.

"Good morning."

"I'd like to check out my house before starting today. I'll go over right after we eat and be back by nine." She picked up her coffee and last piece of toast.

"Take my car, then," said Mike, as he fished out his keys from his pants pocket.

"I'll ask Pat to meet me there. I need to fill her in."

"Yes, I need to call Rachel too." He took the dishes to the sink and set them in to wash later.
He escorted Kit to the door, then reached out and took her in his arms. "See you soon."

It was a beautiful day but nothing could have made it more beautiful, than to find that everything in her house looked as it had when she had left. No damage, no upturned furniture or drawers cast about. Only, the painting lying upside down with the back facing her, the framer's label exposed to the sunlight as it lay on the dining room table.

Kit was glad now that she had had the forethought to put all traces of the wood filler and plastic in a separate garbage bag and not left out on the work bench, leaving nothing for Saulter to find or insinuate.

There was a buzzing vibration coming from her purse. A call. Kit checked and pressed 'open'. It was Mike. "Yes, I'm okay. So far everything looks all right, nothing really out of place. The painting is on the table. You were right, he did get the address from the label. I'm just grateful he didn't destroy the picture. Really … all right, I'll wait for Pat at the front door before exploring the house." She was secretly pleased that he cared, but didn't think there was any further danger. Nonetheless, she would do as he asked and wait for Pat, before checking out the rest of the house.

A knock at the door announced Pat had arrived, eager to hear all the details.

"It doesn't look too bad," she said, looking around the living room. "They didn't destroy anything?"

As Officer Andres had said, her back door had been secured again from the inside. She would have to get a repair man in and possibly a locksmith, but that was a far cry from the damage that might have occurred if Saulter had known they'd taken the frame apart.

"Just the door," said Kit, "but that can be fixed. I'm just glad it's all over."

"Me too." Pat saw the painting on the dining room table. "I'm glad they didn't ruin the painting." She leaned closer, conspiratorially, "So, tell me what happened at Mike's place."

Kit smiled, and hesitated, deciding what she would say. "When we arrived, there was another woman there already." She laughed at the look on Pat's face. "His sister Rachel, she'd been looking after his place. After she left, we got ready for bed." She noticed Pat's eyebrow raise in question. "I had his bedroom and Mike took the couch. Sometime during the night, he came to the bedroom door and called to me, to say Saulter would be coming to the shop to look for the frame. Shortly after that we heard them rummaging through the shop and there were a couple of guys going through the dumpster looking for it."

"Mike heard them on the stairs. We were about to escape through the bedroom window, when the police arrived just in time."

Then on a more serious note, she added. "Pat, he was so brave, keeping us safe. Hearing Saulter so close downstairs, I was scared. Who knows what night have happened if he had broken in with his henchmen."

❖ ❖ ❖

The rectangular plastic sign on the door had been turned around indicating the shop was open for business. Kit found Mike at the back of the store at his work bench, putting the final touches on a large needlepoint sampler.

"Have I missed much? I'm a little late."

151

Mike smiled at her. "You're my first customer, don't worry."

He paused what he was doing and came to give her a hug. "How was your house? Everything okay?"

"Yes, thank goodness. A few things moved around but nothing broken. Thank goodness he didn't see the frame debris we left, he might have been able to put two and two together and think we had the rubies."

"I left Pat with the repair man, so I could get back here."

He gave her a kiss and embraced her once more. "I'm glad."

Kit looked up at him, and smiled. "Okay, how can I help?"

Mike considered. "How are you with an adding machine?"

"Probably better than I am without one," she said, wondering what addition job Mike had in mind.

Mike laughed. "Good. Rachel left me a pile of sales receipts. She didn't have time to get them ready for the bank deposit. Most are credit card and debit card sales but there are a few in cash."

Kit sat at a small table near the bench, where Mike usually did his paper work while watching the store. "Do you have the last week's deposit available so I can see how it's done?"

Mike stopped what he was doing, and went to get his money box and his weekly deposit book. After showing Kit a sample of his previous sales totals, Kit set to work itemizing the sales for the week.

For the rest of the day Kit altered between bookwork, watching Mike create beautiful matted framed art and helping a customer choose some pre-framed pictures for her bedroom.

Just past three o'clock, a police cruiser pulled up to the front-door parking space and a familiar officer entered the store. Officer Anders smiled when he saw Kit.

Mike had just finished framing a puzzle of a medieval castle and was hanging it on the wall behind his workbench when he heard the door chime. A small twang of jealously grabbed his heart as he saw the police office talking with Kit, then just as quickly left as Anders turned and greeted him.

"I was hoping to find you both here," he said. "I thought you'd like to know the RCMP found the owner of the gemstones. They were stolen from a rather high-end jeweller in London. Leitch will probably be extradited back to face charges there." He looked around. "I'm sorry, but if he caused much damage, you'll want to discuss it with your insurance agent, although I'm not sure yet if the two men with him will be brought up on charges."

Mike shook his head. "Nothing really, a bit of glass broken. The rest was just toppled over."

Anders nodded approvingly. "Good." Then he turned to Kit. "Same with your door. I'm afraid."

Kit smiled. "It's being repaired as we speak," said Kit. "My friend is with the repairman now."

He nodded approval. Anders was preparing to leave, then turned back. "Oh, and on a good note, there was a reward for the return of the rubies. I'm sure they will be in touch with you after the trial; until then, they're considered evidence."

Kit and Mike looked at each other, pleasantly surprised. Kit walked Anders to the door. "Thank you for taking the time to come and tell us."

"Not at all. Good day."

Chapter 15

"Okay, which anniversary is this?" asked Pat, giving Kit a look, unable to keep up with the weekly gifts.

Kit arranged the flowers in the tall vase and gave Pat a look. "Two months and three weeks, if you *must* know."

Pat laughed, sitting on a bar stool admiring the flowers Mike had sent. The gladiolas, with their bright orange colour added an extra element to Kit's décor. The cupboards finished in their brilliant white, Kit had set canisters of copper and an orange teddy bear cookie jar that held her tea bags on the counter, along with a wooden breadbin by the stove that contained all her frequently used spices.

It had been exactly eleven weeks since Kit and Mike had first met. Their relationship had progressed and Kit had spent many weekends with her now—boyfriend.

They had heard about the fate of Paul Leitch alias Frank Saulter a few weeks after the break-in. Leitch had faced trial and had been sentenced to prison. The gems had finally been returned to their rightful owner in London, and a reward had been sent by money transfer to Kit's bank account which she promptly split with Mike.

"What time are they coming?" asked Pat.

"The wood arrived yesterday and the builders are to be here at one." She glanced at her clock; it was just after twelve.

Kit's share of the reward was going toward a large deck and pergola that would add outdoor living space to her home. It would take a while but the end result, she hoped would be wonderful.

"Mike's coming to help."

Pat gave her a knowing look. "It's getting serious then, I'm glad. I like Mike."

Kit gave her a sheepish grin. "I'm thinking of suggesting we move in together. Then he could rent out the other apartment."

"Do you think he'll agree?"

"I don't know. It's a big step, and he's pretty traditional."

The front door closed. "He's here now. Don't say anything, Pat." Pat zipped her mouth in a promise of silence.

"Hi, girls. I see the builders aren't here yet? I parked down the street to leave room for them." He carried his satchel and laid the leather bag on the counter, smiling like a cat that had just discovered cream.

"I wanted you to be the first to see this," he said, and opening the bag, pulled out a book. He laid it on the counter so both girls could see it.

"Oh, Mike. It's wonderful." Kit gave him an approving look.

The cover was a stylized rendition of the fisherman's painting. The title reflected all the work they had done since they had first met: Mystery of the Fisherman's Painting, by Mike Reynolds. After their initial response, Mike explained he had written it somewhat along the lines of the events that had occurred during the last eleven weeks, including the life of William Martin and the hidden rubies. Of course, I changed the names of the fisherman's family and as it is a novel, I changed his to William Moore, but everything is based upon our search and experience." He beamed with pleasure, having kept the book as a surprise. "I had two copies printed as proofs."

"Oh Mike, it's wonderful!"

"Congratulations," said Pat, sincerely. "I can't wait to read it." She checked the time on Kit's clock. "It's late, I have a meeting with the upholsterer. I better go, see you later."

"Bye. Call me later," said Kit. She picked up the book admiring the cover. The rich colour of the fisherman's painting. "When did you take that picture?"

"When you and Pat were in here looking at fabrics."

"Well, it's beautiful." She fingered his name at the bottom, admiring the gold colour of the print. "This is about him then; his life, and his … ending."

"His story," said Mike. He took her hand in his. "And ours."

Jacqueline Opresnik lives in Ontario, Canada,
with her husband Frank and Bengal cat Tiggy.
She received her degree in mathematics and
geology from Brock University. She earned
her pilot's licence shortly after, where she met
her husband. Jackie pursued a teaching career
and taught in the Elementary grades.
She has had a love of writing since she
was ten and is just now beginning to fulfill
her dreams as an author.

www.ingramcontent.com/pod-product-compliance
Ingram Content Group UK Ltd.
Pitfield, Milton Keynes, MK11 3LW, UK
UKHW041347100425
5425UKWH00033B/158

9 781777 432829